Historical Lust Desire

Exploration of Intimacy Passion and imagery fiction

stories

Lana Kendra

it wasn't bought for your personal use only, go back to your favorite ebook retailer and buy your copy. Thank you for acknowledging this author's efforts.

Table of Contents

Content Warning

Due to its sexual content, this book is only for those over the age of legal adulthood. There are some topics with a lot of foul language. All of the characters are at least eighteen years old.

Introduction

Are you in search of an exciting and thrilling book to read? Look no further than this extensive collection of Erotic Suspense book. I offer a wide range of genres, including Romantic Erotica, Fantasy, and Urban BDSM Fiction, to cater to even the most discerning reader. Whether you enjoy Anthologies, Westerns, or Paranormal Romance, I have something to suit your taste. My collection also includes Poetic Folklore, Interracial, Black & African American Literary Criticism, and Gothic Horror for those who crave a deeper and darker reading experience. If you're interested in Futuristic, LGBTQ+, Short Stories, or Lesbian literature, my diverse range of options will keep you captivated. Additionally, I offer Humorous, Victorian, New Adult, and College Women's Psychological Mysteries for those seeking a lighter but equally engaging read. Furthermore, My Fairy Tale Collections,

Transgender, Contemporary Western, Bisexual, and Poetry genres will transport you to different worlds and explore a variety of themes. For my Teen and Young Adult readers, I have a selection of European Geography, Cultures, eBooks, Loners, Outcasts, Mythology, Folk Tales, and much more. With such a wide array of options to choose from, you'll never run out of thrilling and enchanting stories to immerse yourself in.

It is important to emphasize that this content is exclusively intended for individuals who are 18 years of age or older.

Historical Lust Desire

Ashley. Doesn't that sound elegant? When people hear my name, they automatically assume I'm a snob. They still believe I'm posh when they hear me talk. I even seem stylish. My dark hair, large brown eyes, and my skin's Latin undertones always gave them the impression that I was an Italian princess.

Actually, I was raised in the East Midlands on a council estate. Nothing about me was particularly exceptional; all I needed was a decent profession and an excellent sense of style in clothing. Yes, I did speak clearly, and I looked good in a dress or a work suit. In addition, I looked like my mother. But I was really just mediocre. identical to everyone else. I attended a comprehensive school and had experience working in a solicitor's office, handling client files and taking phone calls.

However, I did draw notice. And now I was drawing it to

me. A girl named Hanna had developed feelings for me. I still hadn't determined how much of a shine it was. Was she searching for something more, or was it just friendly? Really, I had no idea.

I was usually a male kind of girl, meaning I preferred boys, but every once in a while, just once in a while, I wasn't against a change. I might be easily convinced that I liked sexy things if the girl was right. As much as I enjoyed sucking a ball bag, I also enjoyed playing with a good, squidgy pair of tits. I liked cute. And, let's face it, Hanna was grabbing my attention.

I had no boyfriend at the time. I was honestly never in a relationship. Could a series of one-night stands be referred to as boyfriends? I'd never had a steady one, as you would say. And expanding on the idea, I would have to return to my school days. Nope. I had a lengthy history of hooking up with people just to fuck them. Mostly males, but some girls as well. Not in the sense of true preference. It was really a matter of common sense. Most folks avoided each other. Boys were easier to come by than girls. I didn't require a strong emotional bond. My libido needs to be satiated. Apart from that, I was content to be by myself most of the time.

That's why I took a solo vacation. I have no one long-term enough to schedule my vacation time with. Even not partners. I wasn't bothered. On travels for singles, there was always someone to hook up with. Others, like me, who were itching for a fast hookup before heading out to explore the area.

And there were the natives, of course. Waiters and bartenders were always searching for a gorgeous foreigner. The year before, I'd spent a really pleasant weekend in Paris. The waiter at the hotel had been sultry. Additionally, he had the penthouse suite key.

Yes. same as it is at home. Usually, I could find someone

who was willing to be accommodating when I wanted my hole tickled. That's probably how I was thinking of Hanna. She didn't travel for vacations herself. This was her home. She was aware that I was only here for a short while, and I had no doubt that her preferences were more in line with her own gender. She would, at the very least, satisfy the aching growing in my groin while I gorged on her adorable little face for a few days. She had charm. a small-framed blonde with fair skin barely covered by her short top and skirt, and a perfectly shaped figure.

She was not as big as I was. I looked cuddlier and I was taller by two or three inches. I was by no means overweight. Simply softer. And Hanna seemed to like my curves, for every now and then her hand would stray and explore my knee under the table or brush across my hip.

I still didn't fully understand what she did for a job. All she'd mentioned was bar work and this and that. She certainly had the cash for cocktails. It was sufficient to know that. I was no stupid tourist here to make a quick buck. She had made her payment.

Hanna was from the US. She was interesting just because of that. She was one of those fearless young ladies you see in the movies, the ones who would brave the wild axe killer by herself while wearing only her tight tee shirt and underwear. When it comes to adventure, the attractive blonde who looked fantastic was considerably bolder than she was physically capable of being. That's how I imagined her, anyway. It also seemed intriguing to make her scream. merely in a more enjoyable manner.

Apart from that, all I could see was her stunningly thin legs clad in a small skirt and walking boots. I was wriggling in my seat at the idea of them around my neck while I savored the flavor of her tight, juicy pussy.

She was also impulsive. hopping quickly from one line of thought to another. An seeming boundless stream of energy.

"Let's dance."

That was unexpected. I was finding it difficult not to stare at her tits swinging beneath the loose material of her top because she was up until now eager to converse and lean back.

"Er, okay. Sure."

She took hold of my hand and dragged me into the heart of the vibrant club. Floating curtains that added color to the overhead lighting. The music was performed live, locally, and on unusual instruments.

The location was even more mysterious when the open smoking of hash pipes at the tables filled the space. But at that moment, just this girl was on my mind as she moved sensually, grinding her body against mine and massaging my groin with her arse. I kept my hands low key, caressing her bare arms or her hips, as I tried to figure out how far she would go.

"This country is my favorite; it's very relaxed.

Did you visit the vineyards?"

"Not yet. It's on my to-do list."

"You have to. Rolling hills for miles on end. Greener than you could ever dream.

Free samples are also available. The Chateau is incredible."

I recommended becoming a little more emotional. "Perhaps we could go together." As we moved, my hands were on her arms and belly. Gently caress her to spark her curiosity. I was dying to get my hands on those tits. They were insignificant in any way. However, their dancing was captivating as she moved.

Abruptly, her arms encircled my neck and she fixed her gaze on mine.

"Are you exclusive?"

I smiled.

"As in ...?"

"As in. Do you only do cock?"

direct and truthful. It pleased me.

"Why? Have you got one?"

She laughed out loud.

"I have a plastic one at home if it helps."

I could have kissed Hanna's face because we were that close. There was an exam. She was trying to get me to back off. I declined. Rather, I offered her one last affirmation. I moved my hand over her tit and gave it a little squeeze, enjoying the way it responded beneath my fingers. Not sagging, not too firm. Just perfect. Her smile made me tingle. Soon after, we shared a kiss. a brief, soft kiss that lasted for almost thirty seconds.

Breaking away, she muttered, "The music's crap."

It was that. I was aware. She also knew.

"Just a bit."

She muttered, "Let's go for a walk. Somewhere less... public."

I gave my hand to her. It was my second day here. This worked well. Now that I had someone to spend the night with who would calm the primal cravings turning my stomach, I felt secure. Someone for the next two weeks, maybe?

We stepped outside into the balmy evening. Everything was peaceful except for the sound of stray music and passing voices. The sound of insects might be heard if I listened closely. The sound of crickets or other similar insects chirping. Occasionally, a bird that had made its home for the night would also call.

Hanna continued to cling onto my hand and remarked, "I

was worried I might be making a mistake."

"I thought you might be a cock worshipper. Not open to the alternatives."

We strolled along the waterfront, avoiding the boisterous pubs and clubs.

"I'm either. Whatever takes my fancy."

She smiled broadly and swung my hand back and forth between us.

"I get that. I don't mind a good pounding. But I do have a preference for... pussy when it's available."

She came to a stop and met my gaze with her large blue eyes. Her mouth was grin. I wanted to give her lovely, soft lips another kiss.

To be sure there was no doubt, I said, "It's available."

"No significant other lurking in the background? A boyfriend or girlfriend at home you're going to feel guilty about after?"

"No. No one. I'm a free agent. Everything you see is up for grabs."

Her gaze swept over my entire body, not even trying to cover up the fleeting glance into my cleavage. I felt a child's excitement for Christmas morning all over me.

It was difficult to determine who started it. It was a mutual thing, of sorts. We decided to go for it simultaneously, both of us. We were kissing, mouths open, tongues entwined, before I could really take in what was occurring. Her flavor was quite sweet. Liquid lips and a faint alcoholic taste. The breath was as clean as a summer breeze. Her hands slid up my waist, grazing the sides of my tits, and then down my arms, landing in the cock of my elbows, where erogenous nerves sent shivers down my spine.

We were moving again, somehow. I alternated between pushing Hanna till we reached an alleyway and walking backwards in one second. There are hands everywhere. She pinched my butt, and I had to push against her because I was so excited.

"Ooh."

She whispered, "I so want you."

I lifted her blouse, revealing two exquisite teardrop tits. In my hands, they felt incredibly soft and springy.

There was a hand sliding down there as I felt my jeans pop open. A toasty hand on my stomach, fingers fumbling for...

"Uh."

As her fingers caressed my pussy, I arched my back and pushed my ass out. I saw that as a request to follow suit and reached down to lift her skirt's hem.

She muttered, "You're so wet."

"I like it."

I was surprised to see there were no underwear. Simple,

exposed skin that seeped with smooth honey. supple and cozy. I inserted my finger and moved it back and forth in her pussy. Warm and reassuring.

Hanna gave a cry of "Fuck."

She wriggled with delight. She put more pressure on my pearl and inserted two fingers into me, moving them in a come-hither motion that made me wriggle.

"Oh my god."

The next action was swift. Gasping and moaning with delight, we worked each other out. Fingers on a mobile, moving together to create that happy moment that everyone wants to share with a partner.

I had no idea that I was only a few feet from the main road. Even though it was just late evening, there was still a lot going on, and looking back, it's amazing that nobody saw us in the brilliant moonlight. But I didn't care at the time. Hanna also did not.

We arrived as one.

"Fuck."

"Aw yes."

We trembled on the tips of one other's fingers, holding each other upright.

"Christ."

I moved aside and kissed my fingers, still trembling. Just the taste of her on my lips was enough to pique my interest once more. I arranged my clothes properly.

Hanna let out a gasp, "That was amazing."

She held out her hands and whirled on her heels, and in the silvery light, I could see her big smile.

I said, "Intense."

I was unsure of what to do next as I stared at her. Shall I ask her to come back to my room? I wanted to give her a good fuck. Had I made someone my companion for the next twelve days? Or was she just seeking that fleeting sense of fulfillment? Although I wouldn't mind a one-time exception, it would be more engaging if it could last the entire vacation. My every thought was already consumed by what I could do with that beautiful physique if I had more time.

Hanna took up the space.

She said, "Wanna go to a club?"

"Somewhere special, that tourists don't usually get to see?"

"Okay."

Already, she was resolutely throwing herself down the street.

"Come on. You don't want to miss the main event."

I quickly followed her, stealing glances at her legs as she walked slowly. The way the garment billowed around her, threatening but never quite exposing her pleasure palace, brought out the form of her calves and the tone of her exquisite thighs.

She was such a small thing, with flawless features all over.

She's the girl I desired. I really wanted her.

A pair

"Where is this location?

It didn't appear that anyone could enter this place."

When Hanna had mentioned club, it wasn't what I had anticipated. Like most of the town, it was an old building. unremarkable with nothing to promote its intent. The two muscular bouncers weren't needed because there was no line outside, and the interior was as disorienting.

With pride, Hanna stated, "They can't."

"Only money or looks get you through the door. And if you're brave, looks can get you money."

What was meant by that?

It wasn't the scene of dancing lights that never stopped and the kind of music that made you feel sick to your stomach as you pressed up against other dancers. It wasn't boisterous or noisy either.

Everything was much more muted. More akin to a spacious bar with cozy chairs and tiny tables. Drinking and conversing, groups, couples, and individuals gathered around. Above our heads, cigarette smoke created its own microclimate as it drifted upward. Once more, the cigarette fragrance was combined with the unique hash smell.

Above everything else, though, I saw that everyone appeared to be well-off. the majority being in their forties and thirties. No outsiders much like us. They all wore a combination of more local and Western European clothing, and they were all citizens of the nation or at the very least locals in the area.

There was only one other Westerner, us. And the only ones

with such informal attire. I wondered in my mind how we'd gotten in at all.

Hanna handed me a glass, and I responded, "Not what I was expecting."

"What's this."

"A local drink. Sort of like gin. Careful, it has a bit of a kick."

I took a sip. Sweet. But it almost scorched my throat when I swallowed.

"Wow."

"I warned you."

I took another, more measured drink. It was fruity from the area. lovely.

"The music's not up to much though." I replied.

She smiled and said, "We're not here for the music."

Just as I was going to inquire as to why we were there, the

lights went down and spots revealed an elevated catwalk that I had not before observed.

A group of six cloaked people approached the stage and formed a line. A PA system was used to announce announcements in a loud voice. I was staring at the row of boyish faces in dumb wonder, not knowing what on earth was being spoken. I had anticipated that they would start dancing or that a singer would come on stage. Instead, the cloaks were dropped and unhooked at what I took to be an announcement from the announcer. I gulped in dismay.

A steady stream of youths, all roughly my age. All really beautiful. totally nude. Every one of them proudly strutted down the catwalk, flashing his cock to the onlookers.

"Oh my god. You mean we're here to look at dicks?"

At the sight, I could feel my pussy seeping into my underwear. They all had smooth wax, which gave them an even younger appearance. I observed their balls and muscular buttocks swing between firm thighs. And those cocks, some bouncy and hard, some flaccid, as they went.

"Nice?"

Slowly nodding, I was transfixed by the obvious exhibition of masculinity.

"Yes, screw me.

I would suck any one of those given the chance. Look at them."

Hanna pressed herself against me till I could feel the heat from her body and whispered, "It's not just cocks."

"There's more to come later. But keep watching."

I was obsessed. Gorgeous male genitalia, including cocks and balls, are paired with lean bodies and elegantly sculpted thighs. Imagine having my mouth around those flaccid little cocks as they became hard on my tongue, or riding the erect ones until I came, had my mouth watering almost as much as my pussy.

I failed to stop and think about what was happening because I was so enamored with the obvious masculine nudity. It was a harmless display for my titillation for a few moments.

Squirming up against Hanna, I murmured, "Oh fuck. I need sex again."

"I haven't got a cock, sorry. But I'm happy to help you out again later if tongue and fingers will still do." Hanna said quietly.

Her hand went to my ass and deliberately put her fingers just in my crack, giving it a light squeeze.

"Perhaps with the strap-on if you like."

Arm around her, I didn't take my eyes off the screen.

"I'm holding you to that."

I was trembling while I saw the young males. As they kept circling the stage in a dance, more of their cocks got big. I doubt that I had ever seen such admirable representations of young masculinity.

Then the yelling started. Audience members waved their hands and called out. To stand out from the others surrounding them, women got up. I stared in confusion.

Although I didn't understand what they were yelling, it didn't take me long to figure out what it was—numbers—after I turned to face the raised hands. Cash.

"What's happening?"

I began to doubt the objectivity of what I was seeing at this point.

"Auction time."

I turned to face the men on the stage. Lovely animals that anyone would be happy to carry in their arms.

I let out a gasp when I realized what was going on, "Fuck me."

The majority of those bidding were women. Several

couples, and the odd man. They were making it clear how much money they were prepared to part with for these young men. For the evening, they were purchasing their cocks. Whose wealth got a young man to sleep in their bed?

"Oh my fucking god."

I felt myself grinding my body against Hanna's as she was massaging my ass, eager to have my pussy filled in every way imaginable. That's where I would have stroked my pearl, if I'd dared.

"I find this to be untrue.

It's the meat market, screw that.

I started to regard it as a little soiled gradually. For sex, young guys are selling themselves. However, the ideas hadn't fully settled in. As I watched the display, I was still too thrilled.

Hanna smiled and sipped her glass, "Best meat available."

"Aside from yours."

I smirked, knowing that when we left here, I would receive the fucking of my life. As the young guys lined up for the last bids and took one last walk, my eyes were briefly diverted from the stage.

The winning bidders raised their hands to collect their winnings at the end. Excited and wealthy women picking up the young lads they had paid for. A collar and lead were legally placed around the animal's neck to indicate ownership. It was theater, but they were escorted out to tend to the winning bidders like dogs.

A man was picking up a boy, and I couldn't help but worry if he was inclined that way or was going to be extremely let down by his purchase. A couple had claimed another. The man was eager to touch the fresh skin, much like his wife, I supposed. For an instant, I visualized the delight that young man would experience for the remainder of the evening.

"What happens now?"

When I realized how ridiculous my inquiry was, Hanna grinned.

"Some very rich people get to ride cock until sun up."

"Oh my god."

I was watching, as their ecstatic spouses led them away, toe-curling arses and shapely shoulders disappearing through a side door. I could practically taste the gushing pussies those lovely cocks would soon be buried in, and I could feel the testosterone in the air.

"Aw fuck. Imagine being able to buy willing guys that perfect."

I writhed, barely able to control myself. Right then, I wanted Hanna to give me the finger. to leave me gasping and take away my frustration.

Hanna said, gesturing back to the stage, "Or girls."

"Now watch this."

Then came the gals. It was unexpected, even though I should have expected it. They were beings from paradise. Everyone was equally flawless as the boys had been. They took off their cloaks once more, but more leisurely. Initially, it was merely a tease, revealing their tits only up to the waist. They were then brought to the stage following another round, when I witnessed them displayed to the public in all of their magnificent nudity.

"Oh my fucking god."

Long, silky legs, tits, and silky snatches. Some are bigger than others. They're all so fucking beautiful.

"Don't they look so beautiful?" Hanna muttered.

She had placed her hand back on my ass, rubbing back and forth between my thighs as her excitement was transferred to my groin through her caresses.

It was the same as the boys. Just more males were bidding

this time. Everybody offering a certain amount of local currency to get fucked by one of these girls. The females also gave a round of the stage as they showcased themselves. I scowled at the soft bounce of tits and gazed at taut little asses that swung with every step.

As I thought about it, I got moist. It was simply so completely aroused to see so many cocks and now pussies, and to know that before I went to sleep, they would all be fucking strangers.

"I need to win the lottery."

Hanna bit my earlobe and said, "These people are so fucking rich like you wouldn't believe. The likes of you and me are more likely to be bid for than to do the bidding."

"Imagine that. Being up there. Knowing everyone is admiring your bits and some lucky dude is gonna pay handsomely for it."

"Fuck that. Not for me. I want to be a buyer not a... what are they? Sellers?"

"I don't know. I think it's kinda hot."

"Really?"

Indeed.

Selling yourself, then relaxing as a guy or woman takes pleasure in your body; they want to get the most out of their investment, and the sex will be amazing.

You then pick up your portion of the money in the morning and carry on with your life."

I was watching so much that I hadn't given the reality any thought. Abruptly, the notion that I would be the meat instead of the well-to-do buyer began to shift my viewpoint. These folks were self-promoters. Without the street corner, it was prostitution. All the same, it was sex for sale.

"How much do you think they make?"

"Oh, I don't know. These aren't your typical lads or girls—they're all flawless examples of what it means to be beautiful.

About $1,000 for a single night."

Her hand slid inside my jeans and I shuddered. I writhed against the bar, powerless to stop her fingers from caressing the velvety skin of my pussy.

"Seller or buyer, they all get to stupidly fuck a stranger before going their own ways.

Consider money as a means of introduction, an enabler—pleasure is the main goal, and money is merely a byproduct."

Her fingers maneuvered me with skill. I entered a crowded room and gazed at the most ideal female there was. Hanne.

She sucked her fingers so sensually when she removed her hand. I just kept looking at her.

"Should we leave?" Hanna muttered.

My shakes stopped, and I looked about. The distraction provided by the nude girls and the dimmed lights was much appreciated. I was invisible in my moment.

"Yes."

The club exuded lunacy. An additional cover for global events. prostitute, perhaps more refined and dressed, but prostitute nonetheless. It wasn't my world, though. It had no bearing on me personally. That was what was going through my mind as I followed Hanna and made my way through the ecstatic throng.

I took a long breath of the chilly night air.

"Wow. I'm so fucking horny after that."

Hanna said, "Told you you'd like it."

As we planted a kiss, she stood in front of me. Along with a lengthy kiss that made me gasp and spittle connecting our quivering lips.

I breathed heavily and whispered, "Come back to the

hotel."

I was cum again in the club because to her. After that show, I was still as horny as I had been twice in as many hours. I wanted more than a couple of fingers up my alley, in an alley, because Hanna was looking so damn beautiful again.

She replied, as if it were the most natural thing in the world, "Okay."

I guided her through the late-evening crowds by holding her hand.

My hotel was just like any other. Not much more than an opulent mansion with ten or so rooms. I was on the bottom floor, which had a little balcony. I was fenced off from the softly lit gardens by iron bars.

Hanna flung open the doors to have a look. The air conditioner was instantly overpowered by a burst of heated air.

"This is nice."

"You can see the sea in the distance during the day." I replied.

I was watching my prize while sitting back against the massive sideboard at the far end of the room. With the open doors framing her and the sheer voile blowing a soft, gentle wind behind her, she looked like a picture. Gorgeously sun-kissed legs, paired top to bottom with a pretty little skirt and boots that were way too bulky for the rest of her feminine ensemble. I reminded myself of a skirt that revealed a pantyless pussy dripping with new nectar. She grinned as she turned around to see me staring.

I stared at her while tugging at the fastener that secures my jeans. I pushed them down my legs, not taking my eyes off of them. shaped and fortified by regular running. They looked good, I knew. I unhooked my feet and kicked the clothing out.

Those seductive blue eyes were watching everything. I

then removed my top, pulled it over my head and discarding it along with my jeans. For the first time, I leaned back against the unit and let her see me completely nude save from my thin underwear.

I said, "I think I have nice tits."

I gripped them tightly, causing my dark nipples to protrude between my outstretched fingers. They weren't big, but in my opinion, they had a good shape. I felt my flesh being pushed up between my palms and looked down at them.

"Oh, I agree."

"As good as any on that stage tonight?"

"Oh yes." She said, her voice growing hoarse with want.

I said in a seductive way, "Why don't you imagine you've just bought me in the club."

"Pretend you own me for the night and do what you want to me."

It was still just a game to me, even while I was outside the club and shielded from the forces that motivated those young people to sell their bodies for the greatest price. An exhilarating moment that caused my pussy to scream with need.

"Oh, you're mine bitch. I'm gonna leave you sore. You'll cry for me to stop."

Hanna ripped off her blouse and walked over to me. I caught a glimpse of those stunning tits that I had felt so good about earlier. Now, as she threw her top over my neck like a makeshift leash, they dropped into my hands once more. She drew me close to her and sucked my nipple into her mouth with her lips.

"Uhh."

It felt amazing. I felt a surge of happiness coursing through my body as she shifted to attend to my other tit just as much. My knees went weak and my stomach turned.

"Uhhh."

Hanna dropped to her knees and planted a kiss on my stomach. My panties were pulled to my ankles by her nippled fingers. I moved away from them so she could look.

"Oh fuck me. That's beautiful."

Naturally, my thighs spread apart while she gazed at me. Her tongue then found its way up the length of my pussy, leaving a wet path behind.

"Uhhh."

"You taste divine."

I noticed the big tattoo that covered her entire upper back when I looked down at her. Two dragons from China. With their wings extending towards her shoulder blades, a black and a red creature intertwined down her spine.

Then I felt her tongue part me, and my head fell back. softly pressing and pulling up my damp skin.

"Oh fuck."

Hanna knew her stuff. The thrill of excitement that accompanies a guy was absent. or even the ally way's frenetic finger fuck. Just a long, soft stroke of my steaming, wet skin. She tasted me slowly, as if I were a delectable delicacy. I was a trembling mess determined to give her back the pleasure by the time she got up to kiss me once more.

Hanna demonstrated her skills as a skilled lover in the coziness of a bed. As I crushed my pussy against her ravenous tongue, her hands slid down my thighs and arse before turning to play at its edges.

When it was my turn, I lifted her legs and squeezed them back against her chest, sliding her lovely little snatch in the direction of my mouth, which I vigorously kissed and sucked.

"Uhhh."

I was more thrilled by every groan and every shudder. I could reach out and touch her tits. I kneaded and squeezed them. Her small nipples were twisted until she bucked and moaned. I toyed with her bean after finding it. I sucked it, flicked it with my tongue, and blew on it. She could feel the tiny spot of fire burning every time she touched it.

"Oh fuck."

Approaching, she bucked. A clitoral orgasm occurred. profound and comprehensive. finest kind. The bliss surged through her body, and I felt every spasm of her anus and pussy. Then, unable to handle any more stimulation, she started to push me away.

"Oh my god. Fuck. Stop before you kill me."

She crept up the bed to rest against the headboard, gasping deeply and trembling.

"Fuck."

She called to me as she settled. She cupped my tit, stroking its skin and gently pushing on my nipple while I leaned back against her. I watched as her fingers licked my warm skin between my open legs.

"Uh. Fuck."

Harder and deeper. Up until the squelch of my moist flesh reverberated across the room and her fingers became to a blur. I like having a perspective of the audience. It was an odd feeling to be as arouse from witnessing my pussy masturbating as I was from feeling it.

"Oh fuck."

I arrived with a loud thud. I locked onto her wrist to keep her hand still and in place as my thighs became rigid.

"Aw. Fuck."

The wave of ecstasy ran over my flesh and made me shudder. Again, this hot girl I'd just met a few hours before had elevated me to a whole new level of pleasure.

Hanna propped one knee up slightly and leaned against the

headboard. With her tits propped up on her stomach roll, she appeared extremely erect.

She smiled and waved her lifted knee slightly, "So was it all those soft little cocks being paraded that made you that hot? Or all the bouncy tits?"

"Both. And my just wanting you from the moment you came over to me in the bar."

"Hmm, good response.

I had been observing you for a long time before I approached you since you were so gorgeous in that pub."

That was new to me.

"Really? I didn't see you until you came over."

"I was the other side of the bar, watching you in the mirror. I just loved your hair. So dark and rich."

I went through that with my figures. I felt good with my hair. It was rich and velvety. drying after washing is a hassle, though.

"I just didn't know if you were into girls. I was watching to see who you looked at."

"Who did I look at?"

To be honest, I couldn't recall.

"This one was tough. You were staring at the men, and you smiled extra seductively at the waiter.

I figured you might when I saw you staring at this bitch with her tits hanging out.

I chuckled. That was all I could remember vaguely. a voluptuous female with too-low hanging tits and a huge ass. Not at much my style.

"Don't remember. Only the sweet blonde that came and sat with me."

Hanna had a maniacal smile.

"I was fifty-fifty on whether you were, but I made the right decision."

"I'm fifty-fifty on whether I am. It's the person that's important. Not their genitalia. And you're ... just amazing."

I brought up another topic.

"So how do you know so much about that club? I'm still surprised we got in. We don't exactly look like millionaires."

Hannah smiled.

"since they have an incentive to support emerging talent, and since...

I've been situated there.

I looked in shock.

"You... auctioned yourself?"

Indeed.

Someone bid $1,000 for me in a single night. It's easy money."

"It's prostitution."

I was sorry I snapped that so furiously the first time I said it. I was no judge.

Hanna just smiled wildly, not taking offense.

It's entertaining because the bidders want to obtain the most for their money, which means you get raped like no one else has ever done to you.

Except for the current company."

Her large blue eyes were staring at me as she turned onto her stomach.

"Imagine. For one night you can be a sex slave. Who would know?"

"I'd know."

"Ooh. Sucking and riding a rich man's big cock. You're in a foreign country. One night of extreme pleasure and home with just a glorious memory."

"A woman might bid for me."

Hanna gave a wink.

You don't seem to be having any issues with that.

I believe those ladies have the potential to surpass the men.

A pussy can just keep going, whereas cocks tire out very quickly."

I was wriggling once more. envisioning myself spending a single night as a wealthy man's slave. I thought of the old movie Indecent Proposal. How many times had I yelled, "Take the money," while watching that?

I was fingering myself without realizing it until I noticed where Hanna's eyes were.

"My goodness.

I'm becoming lustful again just thinking about this."

Alright.

I adore the flavor of lustful women."

I watched her face slide between my parted legs as she crept forward. My inner thighs were touched by blonde hair that fell. She then gave me a pussy kiss.

"Uhhh."

Once again I was on that familiar rollercoaster journey towards mental oblivion and I wondered if Hanna would ever cease making me cum.

"It's getting light."

Unaware that she was nude, Hanna stood in front of the open doors. I could see her walking around the club like a procession.

I walked to stand behind her, feeling a piece of her carefree ways spreading to me as I faced it. I wrapped my arms around her waist and gave her a firm hold while digging my tits into her back tattoo.

"The gardens are open to residents you know."

Even though it was early, I cautiously peered about just in

case.

"If we get seen you can ask at reception for a discount. Entertaining the clientele has gotta be worth twenty per cent."

She said, "I need breakfast."

"Get dressed. I know a place that does the most amazing pancakes."

I was tired, even though it sounded nice.

"Don't you ever sleep?"

"Closing my eyes means I wouldn't be able to see your gorgeous tits. Now come on. The sunlight will wake you up."

As I was going to get new clothes, she started scooping up her skirt.

"You can wear something of mine if you want." I said.

I wanted to stop talking about the club. It didn't mean that

I had to accept that the attractive girl I was crushing on was a... take part. Hanna, though, was less eager to let it go.

"Wednesday is the day of the next auction.

Sex shows take place on Tuesdays, the first Wednesday and Monday of each month. These are three days of excitement for those who can afford it."

"Why are you telling me this."

The combination of drink and fatigue had my mind racing.

"Because I'm booked in. Need the dollar."

I was startled with terror.

Yes.

Does that imply our conclusion?"

"No, it makes no sense. It's simply work.

I have to live, so long as you can put up with me having to pay my rent for an additional month."

It didn't make me happy. I knew our stay would barely last two weeks. However, I hadn't anticipated needing to share her at that point. I gulped down another sip of the cool, syrupy beverage. All of a sudden, getting wasted looked like a smart option.

Although I was upset that she would do this, I compared it to having sex with a married man. Yes, that was me. Numerous times. It was hardly uncharted terrain to sleep with someone who knew they were going home to fuck someone else. And it wasn't emotional, at least not with Hanna's arrangement. It was only commercial. My issue was that I didn't usually get emotional about things. After twenty-four hours, I could sense the bond strengthening. I had no idea how to handle that because it was unfamiliar ground.

"You may stop by and visit with me.

And... make your vacation payment."

I gave a headshake.

"Are you fucking nuts? I'm not a prozzie."

"Are you saying I am?"

Hanna appeared insulted, and I felt bad right away.

"No, but—I'm not sure.

I'm not sure what to believe."

"It's just a way to have a bit of fun and pay the bills at the same time."

"And you want me to do the same?"

"I want you to have fun."

"I am. I'm having fun. With you."

I reclined in the seat. I finished. for thirty-six hours awake. Way too much.

"Have more fun."

"It's Prostitution."

"What a harsh word that is.

If you can make things with your hands, you're called a Carpenter and skilled. If you can run, you're called an athlete and awarded medals. If you can model and sell clothes and energy drinks, you're called a model to be idolized. And if you can get your asshole in a magazine, Hollywood will make you a movie star and you'll get to lecture people on Twitter about saving the planet or something like that.

However, when you use your pussy, it becomes offensive. Why? You're merely using a body part, just like you would with your hands or feet.

Why not refer to it as "pleasure therapy"?

She raised her hands inquiringly.

"Only people judging you decide using one body part for work as opposed to another is good or bad. Makes no sense. Who are those people that they can judge what's right or wrong?"

Unsure of how to refute the reasoning without becoming one of those judges, I just looked. I shunned it.

"I need to sleep."

I stumbled to my feet.

"Can you help me?"

I had vertigo. Even with Hanna's help, I never did find out how to go back to my hotel.

She murmured, "Come with me tomorrow." as I closed my eyes, unsure if fatigue or a spinning room would prevail.

I could feel her lips licking my stomach and her hands sliding over my body. Hanna was so energetic, and I was so exhausted. I was falling asleep even as her lips started to glide over the tops of my inner thighs. Would I go to sleep and Hanna lick me? God, that thought aroused so much want in me that I was unable to resist the need to fall asleep.

"Uhh."

I saw those lovely nude beauties in my brain again as her tongue glided gently over my crack. The cocks, too. Oh, those delicious penises are begging to be kissed.

Her finger gently explored my hole like a small cock, "How many men have been in here?"

"I don't know."

I was no innocent, by God. It was very scary when I gave it some thinking.

"Much more than I would want to admit.

Oh my.

I spread my legs wide as her finger began to protrude within. Despite how wonderful it felt, I knew I would not be able to resist falling asleep.

"Ball park figure."

"Oh fuck."

She was stroking my tunnel's neck. locating each and every tense nerve terminal.

"Forty, maybe."

"And girls?"

"A few. Not so many. Ten."

Hell on wheels. That is how high it actually was. Maybe I really was no better than a prozzi.

"And how many were just strangers you picked up on the night? How many weren't passing acquaintances you never saw again?"

I said, "Most of them."

"It's just sex."

As soon as the words left my mouth, I realized I'd lost my own argument.

That's right—it's simply sex.

Will one more then be very bad?"

I experienced a blackout in my head before regaining consciousness. She was accurate. I'd never seen them again after fucking so many people I'd met a few hours earlier. My sexual life was abundant in quantity but lacking in quality. All I saw was a long line of anonymous men and women who let me ride in their backseat and dangled over the headrests. People hardly ever had places of their own, and I never brought them back to my flat. Nope. I didn't even have nice sex. Every time, it was hurried merely to sate an impulse. Maybe spending the entire evening with someone would be more thrilling. Who the heck?

"Okay. I'll do it."

I went to sleep.

That's what I said when I woke up the following morning. Had I really said that?

"God, I'm hung over."

Hanna's large blue eyes were fixed on the pillow beside me, observing. She was grinning, too. I recalled more of my final minutes of consciousness.

"Did you... fuck me while I was asleep?"

"I might have played for a little while. You don't mind do you?"

I smiled.

"No. I don't mind."

It was a tempting concept. provoking.

"I'm just sorry I was too tired to stay awake for it."

"It's okay. I got off looking at your tits while you were asleep."

I laughed.

"Got off?"

She stated flatly, "I masturbated."

"Fuck me. I'd have liked to have watched."

"I could put up a performance for you later.

Now that you're back here, let's take a shower so I can recap what you missed.

I squished my thighs together, feeling my clit grow and hurt.

"Oh my god, absolutely. "

I remembered saying "okay" the night before, and I understood why—anything to get me to sleep—but Hanna was delighted the entire day, and I was terrified. Now she was determined that I would be joining her in her madness.

The problem was that I was unable to locate a good moment to inform her that I would not be doing so.

By midday, I was beginning to doubt my assurance. Could I really accomplish this? Wouldn't it be good to have some cash, almost enough to cover a month's worth of expenses? What would Hanna think if I left her behind?

Considering that she had already done this at least once, it seemed odd that she may be seeking moral support. However, it appeared that way.

"What time is this thing?"

"We need to arrive there by eight.

Although there are just about ten items up for grabs, they prefer to know who will be attending so they can reserve rooms.

"And they're just going to let me join in?"

"I phoned them while you were still asleep. You're in the auction. Don't worry."

I gazed upon her.

"Don't worry? Fuck it, Hanna. You know what you're asking me to do?"

"You like guys. What's the issue? Just have fun. That's all. Don't say that you've changed your mind, please.

I saw that I was examining her closely. Her eyes were

filled with melancholy. The quiver in her mouth. I was overcome with a sudden yearning to win her approval.

"Please Madison. Come with me."

"Not at all.

No, my thoughts haven't altered."

It was truthful. Nor had I. I still detested the concept as much as I had disliked it. I was aware that I would carry it out. for the woman.

"Let's go get some lunch."

I took Hanna's lead and wore a summer dress, skipping the underwear. Walking out of the hotel, I felt vulnerable, knowing that any wind may reveal my pussy to the entire world. It was, nevertheless, also freeing. Though I felt a little rebellious, I enjoyed having no constricting elastic around my hips and feeling free. And there was the excitement. I felt like I was keeping a secret every time a guy looked back at me or lingered with his eyes.

I wasn't sure if it was the heat, the unfamiliar landscape, or Hanna's hedonistic attitude toward life in general and sex in particular, but I was feeling less restricted for the first time. Without the oppressive regulations that seemed to come with being British.

Our choice of eatery was just one of many. A tiny kitchen with outdoor tables. We took a seat with a view of the ocean below. It was joyous. Slender fig trees cast dappled shade against the hot sun. I could see Hanna had a really laid-back lifestyle. I also realized that it required money, even though her actions only consumed a few hours out of her leisure time.

I set down the fork after finishing and remarked, "I do like it here."

It's a wonderful existence.

I'm not going anywhere."

"You wouldn't go back to the States?"

"Fuck that. Nothing there for me."

"Family?"

"A brother, yes, but we weren't close. No, not really.

My mother always had her head in a bottle, and my dad was a jerk who disappeared when I was a child.

No, I'm staying here because, as you'll soon discover, this is a paradise.

I could see it. The issue was that. I found it hard to comprehend the price Hanna's life had to pay, but here she was, content, carefree, and savoring every second.

Hanna removed her shoe and raised her foot while we were seated. I felt her toes move up my thigh and I jolted.

"Fuck, Hanna. There's people about."

My eyes darted about, acutely conscious of our vulnerability.

"Are they under the table?"

"They don't need to be. Anyone can look over."

Her toes wiggled against my bean at my slit. Though I winced, I didn't shoo her away.

I exclaimed, "Oh god."

"You like it don't you."

I looked around and saw individuals ambulating by. Others ate, conversed, and drank while seated at their tables. Nobody was observing.

"Yeah. I like it."

Yes, I did. In such a public setting, having her deft toes rub my pussy was extremely hot. I picked at the last of my food in a nonchalant manner, sitting calmly and trying not to wriggle too much. Knowing that anyone could look over and see what was happening made me scarlet as a beetroot. My desire to get horny kept increasing.

"Okay. Stop."

I adjusted my dress and pulled her foot out of the way.

"Let's take this somewhere else."

"Thought you'd never get the message."

"God. You're insatiable."

"You like that as well."

I grasped her hand.

"Yeah. I fucking do like it. Too much."

I had the opportunity to view Hanna's home that afternoon. a tiny flat above a few stores. Although it didn't seem like much from the outside, the interior was elegant. Moorish wooden furniture and local décor were arranged on cool bare floors. The sun was streaming through wide open windows, and I could hear people downstairs.

"I like it."

"Expensive. Nice places are hard to come by in the heart of town."

I looked at the thick wooden shutters and wondered, "Should we shut the windows?" Not a glass. It wasn't necessary, I guess. The shutters would be sufficient in the event of a storm, and the cold wasn't a problem.

"Nah. They can't look in up here."

"But they can hear us."

Sure, she smirked. "Yeah. I know."

"Doesn't it make you horny?"

"I'm already horny from your toes."

I was waiting for her to come to me, swaying softly and pulling my thighs together to lessen the pain between them.

Hanna tossed her top aside and began rummaging through a drawer. I enjoyed watching her as I saw her tits once more. I could spend all day staring at those.

"I have something if you're up for it."

She held up her promised strap-on, and I smiled. A big

pink object with discreet, thin leather straps holding it in place, resembling a man's cock in shape.

"Aww.

I said, "I'm up for it."

I undid the zipper on my one item of clothing and got out.

Hanna said, "Ooh. You look delicious. Get on the bed."

"Put your butt in the air for me."

It was the first time, to be honest, that I had been fucked by a dildo who was attached to a different girl. I was kneeling with my face down on the blankets and she was kneeling behind me, massaging the tip up and down my crack. It felt thrilling.

As I felt a cool liquid trickle down my crack, she replied, "I like lots of lube." I shivered with anticipation.

"I like to slide in and out with ease."

I shook with excitement.

I huskily muttered, "Fuck me."

"Do you like it in the butt?"

At that idea, I froze. Although it wasn't what I had anticipated, I had played with it a few times before—albeit with actual cock.

I said to myself, "Go for it."

"Ooh. Glad you said that."

That dildo was at my ass, pressing hard against my narrow little hole, a second later. Add more lubricant, and it easily passed past my muscle and inside of me.

"Fuck."

The stretching caused my ring to sting. A nice circle of slight discomfort mixed with the satisfaction of being pierced. And I could feel that massive latex cock getting closer to me. So full, yet so tight.

"Oh god."

It was new to have a large fake cock fuck my ass. To get deeper, I twisted my hips and slid against her thrusts.

"Uh. Uh. Uhh."

Her hand caressed me and stroked down around my pussy as it slid over my arse cheeks in the greasy lubrication.

"Oh god."

"I love how your cheeks ripple when you fuck. And I love seeing your butt with my dildo in it. So fucking hot."

"It feels so fantastic.

Oh my."

She placed her thumb on my pearl and gave it a rub.

"Aw fuck."

"I want to make you cum. I want you to scream so everyone in the street hears you."

I ought to have been appalled. However, I had grown accustomed to Hanna's slighting on the verge of propriety by this point. And to be completely honest, I didn't really care who heard because I was so desperate to cum.

I pleaded, "Then fuck me."

"Fuck me hard."

I could no longer muster the willpower to roll my own hips. I wanted to be taken.

Hanna gave in. She plunged into me, gripping my hips. As hard as she could, over and over again.

"Uh. Uh. Uh."

I could hear my screams reverberating into the street below. What would have been obvious, though, would have been my scream.

"Oh fuck. I'm cuming."

For an instant, my mind raced and all of my ideas were disjointed, causing me to jolt and gasp for air. I was screaming like an animal for a split second. I started giggling then, certain that someone had to have heard me.

"Fuck."

Again, I gasped."

As I regained my balance, Hanna pulled out and shoved her way into my pussy, causing me to fall forward and lose my balance. As I lay prone against the bed, Hanna gave me an even more intense fuck.

"Oh for heaven's sake. Continue on."

This time, Hanna did all the work and rammed that dildo into me until I shouted once more while I lay passively.

Well. Oh. Oh.

Fuck it.

A second later, I was over her, impaling myself in her toy and bouncing maniacally as she reached up to grab my tits. I rode her till I came a third time. I rolled from under her and threw her down to the bed.

Frantic, I went down her body, spreading her legs wide, my mouth at her pussy, my fingers pulling the strap to the side, a pointless hand clutching her phony cock and slickly sliding back and forth in my lubricant and cum.

I was flicking her bean with my tongue and wanking that dildo as though it were real as I stared up into her eyes, and Hanna moaned, "Oh, that's so fucking hot."

I made her cum in my mouth, then I pounded that hole with my fingers and tortured her hot little bean till she bucked and screamed again. I lapped up her cream like the sweet fluids flowing from a peach.

After that, it was so lovely and loving that we laid in our perspiration to heal, our fingers gently brushing against each other.

When I finally get up, I walked carefully to the window, looked out into the street, amazed that no one had heard, and giggled, sure that at least a few people had been hoovering around listening to us in our time.

You're insane. Are you aware of that?"

"And you know there are people across the way who can see your tits." responded Hanna.

I looked up to see the neighboring buildings, their windows facing us with their shutters flung open.

"Oh fuck."

I ducked down and jumped back.

"Hanna laughed and remarked, "You're fun."

"More fun than anyone I've ever been with."

"Thank you."

"We're gonna be great together."

Generally, I fucked someone and went on, forgetting about them soon, but Hanna was reaching deep into my brain and I found myself longing for more. At the back of my mind, though, was the thought that it would only be for two weeks, which frightened me.

And that's why I still couldn't bring myself to tell her that I couldn't follow through with the club. My reticence was slowly but surely giving way; I was infatuated with this American girl and would do anything she asked of me to keep us together, even if it meant hitting on a guy I hadn't met yet.

I was completely lost when I got back to the club; I'd refused to watch the boys beforehand, hiding out the back with the other participants downing more of the local drink; Hanna had stripped off first to encourage me and I'd finally followed suit as the others had done the same; I was quicker than anyone at putting that cloak around me; they all seemed friendly but none of them spoke English; I also assumed that they weren't new to this because they were comfortable doing it; nor was I as convinced that Hanna was as much of a novice as she had pretended; the girls knew her, the organisers knew her, and it was starting to become clear that she was far more of a regular than she had admitted.

I felt a little duped, like my need to fuck her had twisted reality to put me in danger of being raped by an unknown person so that I could maintain her interest, but it was too late now.

Wrapped in my cloak and completely overcome with fear, I stood with the others.

"Now remember."

Hanna continued to talk incoherently and excitedly.

Once you venture outside, there's no way to return. even if all you receive is $50. Don't worry, you won't. Not even if he is attractive. You must proceed regardless of the consequences. You do realize that, don't you?"

That seems a little concerning. Do you know something that I don't know?"

"Not at all. Not at all.

But the folks in charge here. They dislike feeling ashamed.

If I'm making sense."

That gave me a slight feeling of fear.

"Who are those individuals?"

Just... folks that you wish to avoid crossing.

Do not fret. It will be incredible. You'll discover.

Under the cloak, I shivered—not from cold, but from shock.

"Just follow the guidelines. Have fun as well."

I gave a headshake.

"I'm not sure about this."

You'll be alright. Believe me. You don't want to be expressing your desire to withdraw to that guy over there."

I looked. There was a security guy standing by the door in a suit. He seemed enormous. No, I didn't really notice.

"You said I could change my mind right up until I went out."

Indeed. Okay, so I may have overstated a touch.

Unwind."

It was only the involvement of money that made it seem any more sordid than what I'd done in the past. One-night stands were the norm for me, and god knows there had been one or two I'd regretted in the past. Fuck. Too much drink had gotten me into this. And too much blind obsession with this girl's pussy. How bad could it be?

The need growing between my legs was more important to me than social acceptance or even who was answering its call, so I tried not to think about it. Instead, I took a deep breath and reminded myself that at least I'd take some money home with me. Maybe enough to buy a new outfit and enjoy a night out. But then that wasn't a good thing. It made it worse.

I replied, "Fucking hell Hanna." with agreement.

"Hurry up. Simply follow me.

I looked around, hoping to find some fat guy who would pay to fuck me, but to be fair, there weren't any. Fortunately, wealth seemed to guarantee a respectable level of attractiveness. Before I knew it, I was under the lights, staring out into a sea of faces with hungry eyes that wanted to bury their cock balls deep in me.

I told myself that it was like going to a club on a Friday night. Me showing off. Boys and sometimes girls evaluating me. My choosing one to have service my pussy in the back of a car up some dark lane. Different only in that I wouldn't get to choose and I'd have to pay for it.

It was only me who was the newbie, the stupid little tourist led astray by... Hanna. What was she? Why was I letting her corrupt me? How could I feel so much for someone I'd only met two days ago that I'd compromise my morals? I looked at Hanna, who was positively bouncing at the prospect. Then I looked at the other girls. None of them seemed phased. They were like Hanna. They'd done this before.

I began to question if I had morality. I mean, I had so many partners, and I was criticizing this? Maybe this was my worth? Maybe this was where I belonged?

I didn't understand what the auctioneer was saying, and I kind of thought that could be a good thing because I really didn't want to hear someone calling my tits and pussy selling items and treating me like a piece of meat.

My nipples sprung out like little buttons that hurt from their hardness, and capillaries beneath the skin opened, filling with hot blood, turning me red all the way down my arms and to the tops of my tits. My darker tones covered up and evened out my blushes, and under the lights, I doubted anyone could see how coloured up I was. I lowered the cloak down onto my arms like the others did, acting like an automaton.

What the fuck was I doing, I felt queasy?

I was trembling with anxiety, certain that my frail legs would give out and leave me like a stranded jellyfish on the catwalk, but only the atmosphere could carry me.

I had no problem showing off my tits to lovers or even going topless for a beach bath, but it was hard not to cover myself as I walked forward, almost into the throng of onlookers. To expose myself to forty or fifty people with raging hormones and deep pockets was something else entirely, and worse was to come.

When I got to the end of the catwalk, I let the cloak fall to the ground and turned to follow the girl in front of me, shaking with embarrassment and fear. Hanna followed behind me, but all I could think about was the hungry, eager eyes peering over my legs, my arse, my tits that swayed gently, and most importantly, my pussy—a pussy that was already wet and leaking its betrayal onto the tops of my thighs.

I cringed as I proceeded with my round parade of assets, terrified that now everyone could see my small starfish arse hole.

Every step was laborious and took an age, as if I was stuck there forever. Eventually, though, things got easier and my last circuit became less stressful.

When the bidding started, I was picking possibilities and evaluating them according to who I wanted to win, trying to figure out who was putting in offers for me among the many waving hands. It was a cacophony of excited noise that was impossible to follow.

I tried to tell myself it was no different from a Friday night out clubbing, but there was no use in pretending otherwise. One of those faces out there belonged to a man who would fuck me, stick his cock in my mouth and shoot his load, probably in my arse too. And I'd have to do it.

I cursed my own foolishness for allowing myself to be so easily manipulated into this predicament, where I had no say in who may touch or fuck me as they pleased and could not even object.

Every movement, every glance, was magnified in my imagination as time seemed to elongate into an endless anxious expectation; the figures baying over my body moved in slow motion; reality returned with a bang of a hammer.

Men started to move forward, picking up the leash of ownership as they went. I trembled, a mixture of excitement and fear.

I watched and appraised him rapidly as he approached, and when I saw who had proven the richest and keenest among my suitors, I breathed comfort.

His eyes were kind, or at least I hoped they were, and he had the appearance of a wealthy businessman in his early forties. He was Arabic, with thick dark hair.

He murmured something I didn't understand, and I bit my lip a little and smiled nervously before he put the collar over my neck and attached a leash to it.

As he walked me away, I quickly looked around for Hanna. She was already gone, claimed by whoever had selected her. My sweetheart was led away for someone to have a meaningless sexual encounter, but I wished it had been me.

As I was urged on, I looked forward once more and saw a heavy wooden door ahead, rooms waiting for the successful bidders and their... purchases. I felt like an observer to my fate, watching as naked flesh was guided on leads through more heavy doors, watching as giggling girls at ease with what was about to happen. Ahead of me, I saw Hanna, her tiny naked frame slipping behind a closing door, and I knew she wouldn't be mine again until the morning.

We made our way to the room, which was another heavy door in the local Moorish style, and where I would be my owner's slave for the night. The room itself was like the rest of the club, almost like stepping back in time to a time when women were property of and subservient to their male masters. At least for that night, that was the world I was going to live in.

I moved into the center of the room and waited, thinking that this would either be the greatest experience of my life, as Hanna had always assured me, or the most terrifying thing that could possibly happen to me.

The door clicked shut with a loud clunk, and my heart nearly burst. The man, my master, stood behind me, his hands gently stroking my flesh, and I couldn't help but cringe at his touch—a stranger, a man I'd seen caressing my flesh only minutes before. Nothing about him bothered me beyond the fact that I didn't know him, that he was a stranger I'd met less than five minutes earlier, but then, was that really any different from all my previous lovers, who I'd met in bars or clubs only hours before, sucking their cocks or licking their pussies?

I gasped as he gripped my tits, and my hands went to his, just keeping them in place. I was shivering as his hands moved over my thighs and back up to my waist.

"Oh my god."

I trembled as he moved his lips over my sensitive nerves, his breath hot against my neck. Then he started licking my spine gently and kissing my back. I was a trembling mess.

When he bent down behind me, I moved to lean against the wall for support because I thought I might pass out.

"Fuck."

He licked my holes and pressed his face into my arse

cheeks. all the way up around my little brown starfish and all over my pussy.

I nearly arrived there right away. A mixture of his skillful tongue, disbelief at what I'd done, and embarrassment.

I pondered the number of women this man had purchased. How many attractive young women he had paid well to fuck. I wasn't delusional. I was only one of many people who had given themselves over to him. I told myself over and over again that it was the same as all those other guys who had fucked me. Every week, a new female would emerge, and I would be just another one.

When he stopped and began to undress, I was gasping. He was removing his clothes while he spoke. Not a single English word. His voice sounded pleasant and his words were uttered softly, but I had no idea what he was saying. I was positive that his gaze was flattering as it passed over me.

Honestly, I just stood there. I gave him a look. A puppet that obeys and waits patiently. But my eyes were back on him. I was evaluating him, trying to determine whether or not I would have selected him in a different situation.

Hard work, that. Personality is a major factor in our attraction. I was unable to make a judgment on it in such a brief amount of time, especially since we were unable to speak with each other. I had no idea what his name was. I have to admit, though, he did appear fine.

Alright, he wasn't flawless. He wasn't as young as those male slaves, and he wasn't as attractive as most people. a little paunch in the belly, poorly developed pecs. However, not worse than the typical male. superior than some. He wasn't all that horrible. We would fuck like animals meeting in a wild, I thought to myself. I would take it and be humbled. Once we parted ways, I would forget about him and all the people I had been with.

My eyes widened in surprise when he revealed his underwear. I had never seen a cock as magnificent and darkly colored as his. Perfect replicas that I had seen being paraded around the other night were easily matched.

When I looked up, he was grinning. He had caught me glancing. I turned red once more. If it was possible, redder than I already was.

He approached me, reached for my leash, and tugged it slightly downward. It was obvious what was anticipated.

I mumbled, "Oh fuck. Fuck. Fuck." in a hushed voice.

I bowed.

Holy...Shit...

Why did I do that?

I might be a little crazy. I was by no means a nice guy. However, this? It was absurd.

However, here I was. His cock was also visible. Merely a

few inches distant from my visage. It demanded to find a warm, cozy spot as it bobbed at me. I gazed upon it. It was breathtakingly gorgeous. Alright, I persuaded myself, this wouldn't be all that horrible.

The man spoke once more, and I felt another supportive tug on my leash to serve as a reminder of my subservience. Aw shucks.

I shut my eyes, opened my mouth, and covered his crown with my lips. It was only a manhood. Not unlike any other cock that had experienced the pleasure of my lips. Yes, it was superior to most. It was pleasant to feel against my lips. I turned my tongue around his knob, daring myself. Smooth and bulbous, shaped like a little mushroom. I relished it. It had a nice flavor.

I felt more in control as the man let out a beautiful groan. With each bob of my head, I would grip onto his shaft and push it deeper, growing more daring as I slowly began to ride my lips back and forth other him.

I relaxed, going into my sultry state as my excitement grew. I reached for my pussy to try to relieve the pain. I started to lick its underside, ride it with my lips, and tickle his balls with my fingers as I grew more comfortable sucking on his cock. He looked fresh and clean. He was as good tasting as he smelled.

I moaned, "Mmm."

I pulled his bag and ovoids into my mouth and used my tongue to roll them as I sucked on his balls. It was his time to struggle to his feet now. His cock throbbed as he gasped for breath.

He let out a grunt and emptied his lips when I put it in my mouth once again. The cum of a man I'd probably only met thirty minutes before filled my mouth. A man I had never heard of and most likely never would. However, I had signed a contract. I had made a commitment to win his approval, and I couldn't back down now. I ingested.

He seemed content. And yet as enthusiastic. He led me to my feet and showed me to the bed with more meaningless phrases. I lay back and attempted to settle my breathing, heart racing and confused signals coming from every part of my body.

With a leg between my thighs, he bent over me, determined to investigate my tits. Allowing him. I only peered down, snatching tiny breaths while his hands massaged my mounds and then pinched my nipples. I shook when he touched me. At once aroused and terrified.

"Uhh."

I trembled, realizing that I had a role to play in this. an explanation of how I use my pussy to make money.

He kept playing at my tits as I refocused my attention on his cock. It was softer now. I picked up a semi-limp bit of gristle and ran a hand over it. It was pleasant. Wet and gummy from his sperm and my saliva.

He gave me a breast suck. by turns, both.

"Mmm." I prompted her.

Once more, he muttered incoherent phrases.

"Stop talking. Just suck my tits."

I returned the grumble, putting my hand to the back of his head to make sure he understood. As long as I didn't think too hard, it did feel pleasant. I told myself that it was just sex.

He performed it well. The finest. I moved a little bit down the bed to rub my raging pussy on his knee.

"Oh my god."

His lips teased my nipples tenderly as I played with his hair. He reached over to my pussy and rubbed a finger around my pearl between us.

"Uhh."

I writhed and pressed myself even more against his leg. I tightened my thighs around it, squeezing to quell the escalating rage.

"God, I need fucking."

I had completely forgotten about the repulsive nature of what I was really doing at this point. that I was acting like a typical street vendor by selling my body. All I wanted was sex. If it had sated my pussy's hunger at that very moment, I would have fucked a post in front of all the nation's tourists in the center of the beach.

His cock had hardened again in my palm, and he was caving in to satisfy the impulse, scheming to lay over me.

Holding my calf, I raised my legs to allow him to give me a really deep fuck. He was at my door, his meat hanging over me.

"Oh fuck."

The idea of giving myself to a total stranger with whom I

had no sexual connection at all made me gasp once more.

"Uhhh."

More meaningless mutterings, and that steely shaft went through me like a rod of steel.

"Fuck."

It did not build slowly. He thrust instantly, powered by his hips. Swift and ferocious, delivering a rhythmic slap to my ass.

"Uh. Uh. Uh."

Now it was just sex. Everything else didn't matter to me; all I wanted was to fuck.

I allowed him to fill me up to his full length by holding my ankles wide. He gripped the leash forcefully, causing the collar to tug at my neck. It felt seductive somehow, even with its symbolic meaning.

I said, "Oh, that feels so good."

It was. I was confident that, even with the language barrier, my tone conveyed that.

"Fuck me like you mean it."

That must have been successful because he now held onto my ankles and continued to force my legs apart until my thigh muscles and painful, stretched hips protested. As he fucked the living daylights out of me, his thrusts became nearly frenzied. To the amusement of his eyes, I was bounced on his cock, my tits jiggling like jellies on my chest.

"Uhh. Uh. Uh."

I firmly grasped them as I approached. I gave myself a full body tremble and released my nipples.

"Fuck yes."

My body shook so badly that I threw back my arms and took deep breaths. And that cock continued to pound into me.

Abruptly, I experienced the warmth of his sperm growing within me.

The stranger came to a halt and took a deep breath. I briefly fixed my attention on his face and experienced the same wave of panic at what I was doing. Then he was pulling me up and talking before I could answer. I kind of hoped that I could comprehend him.

I was pushed around and forced to kneel before being turned. As he pushed me forward onto my all fours, I understood. I felt a force on the small of my back, causing my collar to snap up and forcing me to arch my back and raise my head.

"Uhh."

His cock briefly rubbed against my pussy before sliding in on my moisture. Leash-wearing dog seemed appropriate as the man fucked me one more.

"Uh. Uh. Uh."

I had my head held high and was pounded hard and forcefully, unable to flee. I was a jerk. An animal in the wild that the stronger male grabbed and held.

I felt as like I was on the verge of an orgasm the entire time. Then a wave of pleasure washed over me, weakening me.

"Uhh."

I came again, and my body jolted, supported only by the leash around my neck. And he filled me with his seed again.

The night was really lengthy. He played with me and my sucking and working his cock for a good portion of that time. It was enjoyable. There was nothing to be gained from that. As the sun rose, he raped me once more, and I was rewarded with a little period of sleep. The day was sunny when I woke up, with warm beams of light filtering through the wooden shutters. My garments had been carried into the room by someone who had left, my nighttime owner. nicely folded at the foot of the bed, as they say.

I walked to the entrance and was greeted by a gorgeous female.

She said, glancing at a diary, "Number four."

My auction number was four. Four was the number on the door of the room and the fourth to be decided upon in the bidding battle.

I blushed with shame as she pulled an envelope out of a pigeonhole behind her, grinning. If she had ever done what I had just done, I pondered.

"I hope you had a pleasant experience."

"I did. Thank you."

How else could I put it? I was still mentally processing it. Striking a balance between the delight and the horror.

"It's fun, especially when you count the money." She

laughed.

Regarding the money, I wasn't so sure. It wasn't really my intention to link the two. However, I couldn't deny feeling happy. What sex always delivered, the night had provided. that sensation of something being lifted. Several hours later, Carrie gets me through a mild high.

Do you recall ever...?

Or do you merely staff the front desk?"

She smiled as she opened the letter and turned to face me.

"I'm one of the fixed-price girls."

I doubt she realized I was confused as I gave her a questioning look.

She continued, "I have college expenses to pay."

They counted out the foreign notes into my hand. In what I thought to be actual money, I calculated twelve hundred. It was thrilling as well as terrifying to think that I was worth that much. What did a hooker on the corner make? Just one? A couple hundred? with inebriated? It also carried a risk that wasn't there. When I gave it some thinking, it wasn't that horrible.

"We keep fifteen per cent back for fees." She stated.

Reasonable enough.

"Thank you."

I placed the cash into my pocket after taking it.

"Sorry. I didn't understand, fixed price?"

Her smile returned.

"The customers that aren't successful. They still need to be entertained. We do that. The very beautiful are bid for. The others, like me, look after the rest of the guests."

"Oh."

I hadn't given those any thought. I guess that was evident. If they weren't guaranteed anything, they wouldn't come from all around.

"It's not so glamorous. Less money and I have to have sex with five or six customers. But it's okay."

"But you're very pretty. Surely you could be ..."

Her smile returned.

"I'm not so special; there are hundreds of people like me who don't get to sell their services.

"I only make a quarter of your worth. European girls are very popular," she added, sounding disappointed.

I gave her a quick glance. She had great beauty.

"I'm surprised. You look lovely."

"Many thanks.

I have to budget for my studies, but it's better for me to know what I will make. It's probably less, but it's steady. I'll make the big bucks when I'm a lawyer."

She grinned broadly.

"You should come again. You will be so popular. They will always bid high for an English girl. Blondes do even better. Like your friend. She is also very popular when she auctions."

"I don't think so. I'm only here for a holiday. Two weeks and back to rainy England."

"Shame."

"I believe you'll be seeing a lot more of my er, acquaintance that lives here.

"I assume she's already a regular?" I asked, trying to gauge Hanna's sincerity.

Yes, she is a really popular girl who has been here for a while.

She is, I believe, the only American who has ever taken part."

That concluded it. She wasn't as innocent as she had implied. I believe I had previously deduced that. Honestly, it made no difference. She had to live, as she put it. And there was no doubt that there was more to our connection than just a business agreement. I forced the thoughts from my mind and went outside to wait for Hanna. A few minutes later, she came out grinning from ear to ear.

She asked expectantly, "Well?"

With a laugh, I said, "It was... amazing."

"See. I told you you'd like it."

I got up.

"Yeah. Well. I need to forget about it now. I'm not a prozzie."

Hanna took hold of my arm and held tight.

Think not of it in that way.

Come on, I need sleep and breakfast.

We can spend the night on the beach when we find a small bistro along the front."

I laughed as I followed her lead.

"You want to sleep on the beach in the day?"

"Yeah. Why not. It's too hot to be stifled up inside. Breakfast, fetch our bikini bottoms and we'll go rent a parasol."

"Bottoms? Just bottoms?"

Hanna continued to smile wildly.

"It's a fucking beach. Everyone's topless. And just think of all those men looking at tits they can't afford."

Though I shuddered at the prospect, I did not argue.

Hanna laughed and said, "If it's quiet, we can have a little play."

"Are you for real? One I'm fucked. Literally. And for two I'm not doing anything publicly."

"Ooh. Public is such fun."

Gazing at her, I pondered what more she had accomplished

that I was unaware of. or her intentions.

"The girl at the club. She said you're a regular."

Hanna glanced down for a time.

"Is that how you pay your way?"

Indeed.

Is it significant?"

She took my hand, and I could feel her anxiety that I might become irate.

"Working fifteen or twenty nights a year isn't worth that much money when you stack shelves at Walmart."

Additionally, this nation is made up entirely of markets and neighborhood family businesses rather than Walmart."

"How often have you carried it out?

Isn't it more than you stated?"

I wanted to know even though it wouldn't matter.

I've lived here almost two years, so I'm not sure. Usually, I come here once a month.

"Christ, Hanna."

Look about you. My home is a heaven. But the price is high.

How else am I going to cover my food and lodging costs?"

And you're at a loss for what else to do?"

Actually not. How would I respond? Pour coffee? That wouldn't cover my rent at all."

It was bar work or something, and I couldn't really dispute with her; what could a foreigner do here?

"And you refused to return home?"

"I informed you. I also didn't find anything there. And this location is a utopia."

"How about in the long run? What happens to a chubby forty-year-old?"

She appeared appalled.

"Sick? That is not going to occur. But my bank account will be well-stocked by then. I'm not a moron. I preserve."

My mind was racing with wild ideas; it was getting difficult to believe that in just one more week I would board an airline and take off without this girl; it was also getting harder to believe that I was falling hard for someone who made her money by fucking random people.

All of a sudden, she said, "Stay with me."

I gave her a skeptic's glance.

"I'm unable. There isn't a work permit for me. My stay is limited to ninety days."

"You think this place is concerned with employment permits?

Despite having been here for two years, I don't have one. With so many visitors and foreigners in the area, I simply fit in. Nobody is concerned."

"Where should I reside?"

"Uh... Pay close attention.

Remain. Alongside. I.

I enjoy having sex, even though I'm not getting paid too well.

I ought to have realized it was apparent."

I flinched.

"Do you mean that we ought to be...? within a partnership?"

"Are we not?"

"Yes, it is. But I considered it to be a festive custom. I had not anticipated..."

Hanna's disappointed expression made me realize that she truly thought we were more than just friends. To be honest, I wasn't opposed to the concept, no matter how ridiculous it seemed.

"But..."

My mind raced with possibilities, but I shook my head, calling it craziness. I would be a prostitute no matter how I dressed, and it was the only way something like that could happen to me if I adopted her insane lifestyle.

I gave up and yelled, "Fuck."

I'm not sure if I could pull it off. Though I really want to be with you."

Hanna threw herself over the bed and embraced me.

"So remain here. Accompany me. I don't care how you pay for it. Keep it out of your mind. per month, a few hours. It's that simple.

Please come on. It must be more advantageous than doing a job for a living."

"I would be working." I replied, taking another look at the cost.

"Several hours. I would like to remind you of the great few hours you mentioned. It's one big, never-ending holiday for the remainder of the year.

Sitting on the beach, enjoying delicious cuisine. enjoying fantastic sex with me."

She smiled.

What happens if there are no more bids? There's only so much wealth in the world. A thirty? At most fifty people there. They will desire new girls."

"There's other things that go on in the club if you're adventurous."

I rolled my eyes, trying to look scared.

"My goodness. What are you currently attempting to persuade me into?"

"Not at all bad. On nights out, how about a little dancing? They are publically open every Thursday."

Knowing it wouldn't be so easy, I waited.

"Topless dancing pays good money."

"Topless." I said again.

I gave that some thinking. A week before, I would have said categorically, "No." There was no chance. But now that I'd paraded myself nude on a catwalk and wealthy people were bidding to use my pussy, could I say the same thing?

"And can you imagine the amount of money we could make by staging a show together? Not that I mean to really do it. Simply touching and dancing together.

Getting compensated to perform our volunteer work here."

I couldn't help but realize that Hanna was more than just a romantic holiday crush; yes, I would go to any lengths to be with her, even though she was a perverted little creature. My jaw dropped open.

"We'll start with just the dancing if it's okay with you."

Fucking hell, what was I doing, agreeing to dance with my tits out, and then I saw that gorgeous grin and those eyes, and it just didn't seem possible that I wouldn't do whatever it took to stay with her.

I sat there in silence, taking in what she'd said. I told her about the forty guys and the girls I'd slept with. It didn't seem like much spread over the months and years, each just turning into another fun moment, but at the end of the day, it was a lot. More than Hanna had just admitted to, and I was the one criticizing. It was a number that would easily double or triple if I carried on with my lifestyle, and what would I have to show for it? If I kept going as I was going, that's for sure. Hanna had a bank account, and all I had was an embarrassing body count.

I exhaled.

When the truth hit home, I answered, "Perhaps you're right."

I thought about it and reasoned, "If I do it both days, that's only twenty-four men a year."

If not... About twenty-four thousand bucks. I suppose that's twenty thousand pounds.

Additionally, its value far exceeds that of home."

"Yeah."

She was right, but I still wasn't thrilled about making the financial connection.

"Dancing could help you save almost all of that. That will cover our daily expenses on its own.

Plus, two can live there for less money."

I hesitantly nodded, finding it impossible to argue with the figures.

She tried to sell me on the notion, saying, "And the sex is amazing."

"The customers? even ours?"I smiled.

"Both."

She rolled over on the bed and kissed my tit, licking my nipple softly till it hardened.

Don't leave. If I could never again suck your gorgeous, delectable tit, I would be sad."

I felt her tongue tease my nipple proudly as her lips around it one more.

"Fuck."

She flicked it like a rubbery spring, and my head fell back. Christ, I wasn't sure I could bear the thought of never having her do that again.

So there I was on Thursday, in the same club, with different lighting and loud cubbing music, surrounded by a mix of Westerners and locals, holidaymakers drinking and dancing, locals taking in a taste of a lifestyle they saw on TV, people from closer to home just having a good time, and me, in the middle, on an elevated platform, gyrating in my skimpy underwear and nothing more, thirty minutes on and thirty off, while other girls, Hanna included, were going about my rounds around me.

I was nervous on my first dance with the crowd, but on my third dance, I was completely engrossed in the music. Yes, people were watching me, but they weren't seeing me as a person; I was just background noise. In my opinion, the club had become no different from any other, save for the fact that I was alone and free from prying eyes and guys trying to make out with me. I focused on the music and danced, loving the freedom that came with being nude and not having to wear clothing against my skin. It was almost thrilling to do something I enjoyed, but with such freedom.

It was just a fun evening for me doing what I did on a Friday or Saturday night at home. Okay, so I didn't have my tits out in the high street club in my home town, but I also was constantly pushing guys hands away or figuring out which one I wanted to end up in the back seat of a car with. No, this was just dancing for dancing's sake. It was no big deal. And if anyone was staring at my tits, I wasn't noticing. It was just a fun evening for me doing what I did on a Friday or Saturday night at home.

I did cover up during my breaks so I could sit at the bar and have something refreshing to drink. A couple of guys tried to strike up a conversation with me, but I just smiled and waved them off, not really understanding that I was a clubber and not one of the dancers. That was how much people noticed me up there, really, just a pair of tits.

When it was Hanna's turn, I saw that her fair skin and hair glowed golden under the lights, making her look like Tinkerbell without the wings, her tiny frame wraithlike as she twirled and swayed. I looked around, and nobody seemed to be watching; a few people stopped and stared as they passed, but most people were too preoccupied with their own amusement to notice the girls dancing, so really, it was just me staring at Hanna's gorgeous tits as they swung across her chest with gentle bounces.

When things started to settle down, I noticed a local girl with large tits stepping from the platform I'd been assigned. I checked the time, finished my drink, and skipped across, tossing my top to the side as I got on and grabbed up the beat again.

After a further hour, the venue was beginning to thin out. I used the restroom and changed, emerging from it looking no different from the other patrons save for my dancing attire, which included a tiny shoulder-length robe tucked in with cosmetics and a brush for my hair.

Thus. How did that go?As we made our way back to her apartment, Hanna was clearly having a good time.

"First frightening. However, no. It was alright.

I wrapped my arms around Hanna's waist and lunged at her, wanting nothing more than to be with her for the moment, even if it was certainly not as scary as what I'd

120

be doing on the first Monday of the next month.

"Come here."

She squirmed and laughed as I planted a kiss on her.

"I'm done with flashing my tits at strangers for today."

She grinned and said, "Good."

"Let's get home and you can flash them for me."

"Why hold off for so long?"

Then I dropped it quickly and ran ahead laughing; a week ago I would never have done such a thing, but Hanna's crazy spontaneity was rubbing off on me. Of course, a week ago I wouldn't have danced topless or sold myself to a stranger for sex. A week ago I had been a different person. I stood back and lifted my top, holding it up as I glanced past a staring Hanna for any eyes that might turn my way.

"Relax. Wearing these shoes, I can't run."

Though Hanna wasn't as used to heels as I was, she was

still running after me.

"You gotta keep up if you want my pussy."

I fluttered my skirt upwards, not wearing underwear, since it had become my usual attire.

When I dropped my skirt, a couple of females who had heard what I had said chuckled and looked back at me. I wasn't sure whether they had seen my snatch, but it didn't matter.

I waited for Hanna to catch up, and then we joined arms to complete the last distance.

You will adore this place. We'll age together in heaven and have the best time ever."

Hell no, Hanna. I'm 23 years old. Years remain before I start to worry about getting old."

Twenty-three, huh? You're really old."

Why? When were you born?"

"There are 21. In a month."

"Shit. "You're a baby," I gave her a strong hug.

Indeed. You're accurate. Years yet. However, I like the thought of growing old together. Maybe one day.

When I'm fifty, will you still want to have sex with me?"

"At fifty, sixty, or hundred years old. Every ten minutes."

As we ascended the stairs leading to her flat, we couldn't stop laughing.

"Those guys in the club won't bid so much though." I said.

"We'll have to pay them to watch us parade."

We were all over each other in the room; it was a paradise that we were living in, but Hanna was the one who turned it into a true paradise for me. I was in love with her, and I wanted to be with her all the time, to have her make love to me all the time, and to always want her body whenever I looked at her.

"You have that toy with you?I questioned, pulling at her clothing and giving her a violent kiss.

"You want me to ..."

"Not at all.

I'm game for it. I smiled, "I'm going to fuck you like a man."

"Aww. Kindly. Go all out."

I took the strap-on and put it on, standing with the dildo pointing out in front of me while she was rummaging through the drawer.

"Shit. Having a cock must be uncomfortable."

It jiggled as I walked about the room, swinging my arms like a large, strong man as I went from side to side.

I turned and pretended to wank while Hanna was rolling around on the bed laughing.

Well. Oh. "Oh."

I make deep fake tones while extending my hips.

"Oh Madison, my gosh. You're such a bad guy. Never switch up your sex."

I paused and tightened my grip on my nipples, pulling to relieve the increasing pain there.

"That is not possible. These pups would be missed. You know, it took them a very long time to grow. roughly 14 years."

Hanna looked at my tits and her voice grew softer.

With sweetness, she said, "I'd miss them."

"Are you going to dance now or fuck me?"

With a sly smile, I stepped toward the bed.

"Do you want it in your arse or your pussy?"

Hanna was contorting, getting down on all fours, and wriggling her behind toward me.

"On the behind.

lubricants adjacent. Utilize a lot."

I was about to fuck her tight little hole with a strap-on dildo, and I couldn't wait. I was staring at her small pink ring, which was another first for me. Only a finger had ever squeezed through that barrier on a lover before, and never on a female.

Over the next few weeks, I accepted Hanna's hedonistic outlook on life as fully as possible, and when my flight home finally arrived, I embarked on my own journey of becoming an undocumented immigrant, following in her footsteps. She was correct; we were not claiming anything from the nation, we were not taking jobs from anyone, and nobody gave a damn.

I soon forgot how we were going to pay for this lifestyle. The dancing was simple, enjoyable even. I was comfortable having my tits out, as I did most days at the beach. I also rarely wore much clothing as I adapted to the heat; panties, thongs, and bras all lay forgotten in my drawer as I opted for summer dresses, skirts, and loose tops. I was pretty sure that most of the local girls I saw had similarly aired pussies, since it seemed the sensible and hygienic thing to do in the heat.

The only thing that bothered me a little was the extra thing I would have to do at the start of every month. Hanna accepted it, saying over and over again that it was simply part of her job, and as the days went by, I came to believe that was all there was to it.

The modest coastal town was engulfed in a carnival atmosphere as a large festival took place over the course of one weekend during the peak of the tourist season.

We coasted from bar to bar all day, taking in the parades, which featured floats shaped like enormous, colorful birds or commemorating something related to the sea, as well as throngs of skimpily dressed dancers making their way down the street. It was one big party that we, along with everyone else, joined in on.

Hanna remarked, "They do this every year."

"The music goes on into the early hours."

Another float caught my attention; it was a huge floral wine bottle with nearly nude girls dancing around inside.

"That's from the big vinyard outside of town." Hanna replied.

largest in the nation. The majority of the wine served in taverns comes from that region."

That night, Hanna treated me to a private little concert in her room. The music was a kind of local sound, coming in through the window from a band that continued to play in the square as the sun sank below the horizon. But what really caught my attention was her sensual dance move.

I settled into a chair and watched her perform like a lap dancer for me.

Hanna raised the skirt, swinging her hips as it rose gradually. And then, just like that, she had a glimpse of her pink tiny pussy before it vanished once more.

Will that be done on Thursday?"I inquired.

Cannot. No sex is permitted."

She pivoted and wriggled her posterior just before my visage.

But surely you would, don't you?"I squeezed.

It is only a body. Everybody has one."

I smiled at her little nipples straining through as she twisted again, lifting her top and twisting and holding the cloth to make it wrap snugly around her tits.

She dropped it a moment later and leaned over to shake her head, revealing her gaping top and letting me see those tits swinging beneath her hair.

"Oh fuck that's hot."

As the band reached a crescendo in their performance, Hanna kicked her legs, swishing the skirt with her legs and giving me more little glimpses of her bare ass and her crack.

She stumbled onto the bed and turned onto her back as the song came to an end.

Do you want to know my daily activities prior to seeing you?"

Was it collecting stamps?"

I did what she said and settled into the bed's corner.

"Not at all. Nothing there to lick. Not very often, anyhow." She smiled.

Her hands were raising the skirt once more, as I noticed.

"You realize how difficult it is to locate girls who enjoy having sex with other girls?"

I did; it was not difficult, but the number was lower than

what campaign organizations and social media would have you believe, at least if you were looking for the prettier ones.

"I was so frustrated."

Her skirt was around her waist, and as she dropped her knees to reveal her pussy, the top slipped off, giving me a clear view of her lovely, beautiful little mound, all pink and fresh. I squirmed as my heat increased.

"Me alone. alone with myself."

I just looked in quiet, taking in the vision as her hands teased her hardening nipples and gripped her tits.

"I had to make my own entertainment."

Slowly, two fingers caressed her crack, gently stroking the velvety heap of her vulva.

Would you like to know how?"

I stared at her fingers, at the wet skin under them.

"Yes." I huskily said.

A finger glided over her incision, opening it and allowing the initial drop of her seeping juice to combine with the perspiration enveloping her form.

"Just like this."

I watched her masturbate silently, frozen in place. I'd seen this on porn sites countless times, and I indulged in it frequently enough every week, but there was something special about witnessing another real, breathing girl sultry.

"Uhh."

Her expression softened, her muscles loosening up as her attention shifted to her crotch.

She teasingly said, "I've tried all the local fruits up here."

"The juicy ones are the best."

Her fingers dug deeper into herself, stroking, and the idea of sucking away at a mixture of citrus fruit and her sperm made my mouth water.

"Uh."

Her bean, which appeared like a little button and was exposed to the room's colder air, was pink and crinkly and wet, and Hanna used her other hand to hold her flesh open for me to see.

I took a quick look at her tits, which were slightly swaying as she rolled around on the bed.

She mumbled, "I'm so fucking horny."

She put both hands on her pussy after squeezing one of those soft, squishy tits.

Hanna's fingers spun faster and faster, her eyes closed, her face still, her gaze turning inward, her attention solely focused on the sensation that was swelling between her thighs.

As I looked, her fingers fucked her little, tight hole, and she rubbed her flaming clit to the brink.

Hanna jerked, bouncing all over the bed, her thighs taut, her small toes pointed straight, her eyes wide and open, and I saw the contractions that grabbed her pussy extend up her abdomen.

"Uhh."

Squeezing every last pleasure from her sex, her jaw hung down as she continued to stroke herself.

She made a small, self-satisfied giggle as she gazed up at me, seeing me again, and then she relaxed, letting her fingers slow to a delicate caress that spread her wetness around.

She said, flashing a seductive smile, "I like being watched."

I released a breath that I was holding but hadn't realized.

I said, "You're so beautiful when you cum."

"Your turn."

I laughed.

Do you wish to witness my masturbation?"

Sure, I'd touched myself while fucking, but to do it for someone else while they were watching—fuck. I'd never done it for anyone before.

Indeed. All I want to see is you cum by yourself. I'm curious about your appearance throughout your most personal times."

I smirked, realizing that I needed it after watching Hanna, and that if doing so was the only way I could get off, then I would.

"Okay."

She shuffled up onto her knees and waited like an eager child at the foot of the bed, while I undressed and took the bed.

"Shit. It's awkward, this."

I writhed as I began to touch my body, starting with just my belly and working my way down to my underpit.

Why?

There's no shame in me when I fuck you.

"That's different."

I spread my feet and massaged the tops of my thighs, tickling them as I did so. Next, I formed circles on my tits, around and around, closer to my nipples.

"Mmm."

I gave my vulva a gentle tap on the top of my pubic bone to let her know I was approaching.

"Uhh."

My palm made a peace sign, fingers caressing the mound around my slit, pressing lightly to squeeze my labia together, and my bean leaped, sending a pulse of joy up my spine.

"Oh my. I'm really, really wet.

I slowly pulled back the hood over my bean, exposing it to cooler air and Hanna's hungry eyes, and licked a finger to wet it before softly stroking it back and forth.

"Uhh."

To avoid racing to the finish, I switched to little circular motions. She wanted to watch. I wanted to enjoy my pleasure. No, I would take my time. The humiliation had gone. It no longer felt unsettling to have her eyes on me; it felt necessary. I wanted her to see me.

I grinned as we locked eyes, feeling ecstatic from both the orgasmic ride and having my beloved curled up next to me in our own little heaven.

I placed my finger at the base of my vagina and slowly pulled it up, not too deep, just deep enough to gather the fluids that were soaking my entire groin.

"Aw fuck."

I could no longer control myself. I was riding the rollercoaster to its peak, speeding into...

"Make yourself cum."

Hanna murmured.

"Cum while I watch."

That wasn't up for debate at that point; I was going to do it no matter what.

"Uhhh."

I spread my other hand madly over my bean and my finger dug further to discover my urethra.

"Shit. Ick.

Fuck it.

My vagina pounded as I approached, and my arse button tightened repeatedly. Hanna was watching at me closely, taking in every exquisite detail. I suppose I passed out from sheer bliss, a total joy that extended to my fingers and toes.

After that, I was back on Earth and was overcome with happiness as endorphins held my body in check. A broad grin of contentment appeared on my face.

"How did that go?"I inquired.

Hanna continued to stare at the silky mess between my thighs, where my fingers were still playing.

"Oh my god. That was really, really lovely."

I let her finish admiring my arousing pussy while I waited, and then all of a sudden I grabbed my thighs and rolled out.

Alright. That's enough." I laughed as my shame reappeared.

I got out of bed and moved to the window to stand.

"Phew."

I cooled myself by waving a hand.

"I'm all hot and sweaty now."

"I've never watched a girl masturbate before." Hanna replied.

"I fucking loved it."

"You weren't so bad yourself."

A peek over my shoulder revealed a busy street, people going from bar to bar or back to their homes and hotels, groups of Western lads laughing loudly and girls screaming, locals shouting to get their attention and inviting them to spend money in their establishments. The band below had packed up, but music continued to drift from further along the road.

I was bending over the frame with my tits hanging down, still at the window, when Hanna came up behind me and shoved me forward."

"Hanna." I objected, fighting to free myself and return to the chamber.

I could see all those individuals circulating below me. Any

of them could raise their eyes.

Hanna did not waver.

"Live dangerously."

Her hand was slipping back and forth between my thighs, rubbing my pussy with its side.

"Fuck."

I tried to pull away again, but she wouldn't let go.

"Someone might look up."

I returned to grasping the frame after attempting to cross my arm over my chest but feeling shaky.

"Don't make a noise then."

She slapped a palm on my mouth and crushed herself against me. She started massaging my heated body with her fingers in my pussy.

Glancing over, I observed the other windows. Squares of darkness that might have concealed a multitude of eyes staring back at me. If they had looked, they would have seen me in the room, but what was different was when I was hanging out of the window.

She said, "I'm going to make you cum again."

I prayed no one would look up and see those fingers moving back and forth, fucking me and rubbing against my pearl while I looked down at the throng.

"Are you horny?"

I said "Mmm." behind her hand.

"You want to cum again don't you?"

"Mmm."

God, I was dying to cum. Why couldn't I? I could still clearly remember the delight. My bloodstream was still racing with pleasure hormones, but they were getting weaker. I yearned for that intensity to return.

Hanna stepped up her assault on my pussy, digging her

fingers deep till my fluids were forced out. The sound of her palm slapping my behind reverberated across the room as the wet flesh squelched. It sounded a thousand times louder in my imagination. There was a loud sound that I was certain was coming from the street below.

gosh, oh gosh. I was being fucked, and any second now there would be a crowd of people cheering me on, watching my tits swing and my wild ecstasy.

"I fucking love your pussy. So tight and wet."

The closer I got, the weaker my knees grew. All that kept me standing was Hanna and the window frame.

"I fucking love feeling the clench around my fingers."

I let out a cry that came out louder than I had anticipated, and that's when her hand left my mouth.

"Fuuck."

Everyone looked up, but Hanna had moved aside, so I tumbled backwards in time and landed on my ass under the glass.

"You bitch."

Hanna was going crazy.

Her response was, "Sorry."

"But you're always at that window. I couldn't resist."

I couldn't contain my laughter.

"I'm nailing it shut tomorrow."

I returned to the club on Monday of the next month. Hanna and I together, holding hands. I justified it this time as a night's labor. Similar to stocking retail shelves or managing client accounts. We stayed in the bar for a while, watching the young men parade themselves and the bids come in. I wasn't as nervous.

I was horny by the time I got backstage and took off my clothes. I was drenched and itching to get fucked just looking at all those youthful cocks. Now I had made up my mind. I would dance on Thursdays and do this twice a month. It was a job. Not a lot more. However, work was well compensated, and I could enjoy the remainder of my time.

We spent entire days eating and drinking, lounging on the beach, or enjoying the finest possible sex. I didn't even somewhat miss England. And in this lovely country, it never got cold, not even when it poured. When it occurred, I relished getting soaked. I enjoyed dancing in the rain while Hanna supported me and my slender dress clung to my body, almost sheer.

But work was on Monday. I would parade and entertain the one who paid the highest. Not out of love. We had sex. a biological function, in Hanna's words. All I had for her was love. It was quite touching. Even though it would be fun to get fucked by a stranger, I was only completely happy when I was with Hanna.

When the cloak lowered this time, I felt secure. I felt no shame about being nude on stage. I was aware that I looked excellent and that I was making the curious audience hungry with my gaze. I experienced heightened perceptions and a greater awareness of my body. But it was a positive experience this time. I remained composed and was thrilled that so many people were interested in me.

When I discovered who had won the offer on my behalf that evening, I was a little surprised. As her guy fastened a collar over her neck, I turned to see Hanna grinning at me. My bidder had not escaped detection.

I turned to face the elder woman, whose big, brilliant eyes were staring back at me as another collar wrapped around my neck. She was maybe forty years old, but she still had a lovely face and black eyes. Her skin, which was a deeper color, was flawless and had just the beginnings of wrinkles around her eyes. They enhanced her unique attractiveness in some way. She looked happy with herself, her lips full and glossy as she led me away with a slight tug.

I glanced down at her body as I followed. Fit was she. Formly. A affluent woman covered in layers of regional clothing.

I was number six this time, and as the door closed, this woman turned to look at my nude body.

"You are English, yes?"

The fact that she understood me made me happier. The fact that I could talk to someone this time around was preferable. that she could tell me what she loved and that we could strike up a conversation.

"Yes."

"You are very attractive."

With the savage grace of a predator, she swung her fingers around my hips and down my back.

"Thank you."

"And are you comfortable making love to another woman?"

She turned to face me, began removing her clothes, and started.

"Yes. It's not ... new to me."

As she exposed herself, I just stared. Huge nipples with massive tits perched high on her chest. She had lovely legs and broad hips. Her pussy was framed by a little bush that limited my view of the surrounding skin.

That's excellent.

I enjoy a girl who has the ability to win over a lady."

She backed away and crawled onto the bed, letting me view her slit before rolling over and landing on her back. She spread her legs wide and extended her hand to me.

I inhaled deeply and moved in her direction. I put my face between her thighs and told myself it was work. Wonderful work.

As I put feather-like kisses on her inner thighs, she remarked, "Such soft lips."

I gave her a harder kiss and licked her flesh to make her feel tickled. I shifted up as I sensed her trembling. My tongue licked the space that separated her vulva from the top of her thigh. I inhaled the aroma of her next-door sex. lovely. earth-like. feminine.

"So gentle."

She reached up to my head and wrapped her fingers around my hair. For the first time, I ran my tongue over her slit as it slowly guided me onto her pussy. I had already tasted her fluids.

"Uhhh. So wonderful."

I put out my hands and caught those tits. I gave them a light squeeze, and they filled my hands and spilled out around my fingers. I trembled with pleasure as I pushed my tongue further along her crack.

"Oh, I see.

Continue doing that."

I reached down further, parting her malleable skin and licking the nape of her neck. I could taste the sweet juices covering my tongue and felt her thrills.

I fingered her and put my hand back down. I moved slowly and deliberately, sucking at her flesh as I felt her muscles tense in certain places.

She turned us around somehow, and I ended up on my back with her laying across my length. She started working on me as soon as I raised my head to see her delicious pussy once more.

"Uhmm."

Her skill lifted me and had me writhing beneath her, slow and precise.

"Uhh."

I gave myself to her, wanting her to eat me alive, and my legs came up, hooking over her back. I could feel her silky pussy on my lips, and it felt amazing.

We paused and shifted positions just as I was about to cum. We scuffled. It wouldn't be so simple without experience, but I'd done it several times. And this was clearly a woman had more than one. Grinding ourselves together took work, but it was well worth it to look into her eyes and feel my heat build up.

She held my gaze and said, "That's so good."

"Such a soft pussy."

I was swaying from side to side while clinging to her shoulder. Her tits wavered in front of my eyes. Large, thick nipples with a rich color aimed in my direction. I was not sure if I should look into her eyes or at them.

"Ahem.

I mumbled, "I think I'm going to cum," as the sensations

in my crotch appeared to build to an uncontrollable crescendo.

My leash was gripped tightly by a hand that kept me standing. I was inches away from her face. As she released them, I could hear her labored breathing and smell her delicious, used air.

"Oh god."

She said, "That's it."

"Cum."

Her hips compressed our pearls together with greater force.

"Look at me. Let me see your soul as you cum."

I was at my breaking point.

"Uhhh."

I lost my rhythm and shuddered as a wave of ecstasy swept over me as I stared into her eyes. I came in force. Maybe an hour of deliberate play had brought me to this level, and all of a sudden, I was bursting with sexual energy.

"Fuck."

She pushed me back into the bed, sitting across my face with her wet, sodden pussy pressed to my mouth, and I was still in that dead zone where my head could not connect to reality. When my tongue made contact with her bean, she approached.

"Uhhhhh."

Juice covered my chin and filled my mouth as it fled from her like I had squeezed an orange. I gulped it down and desired every last drop of her essence.

Following that, we laid close to one another and caressed and stroked each other's hair. We kissed every now and then, and I took advantage of the moment to twiddle one of those large nipples or pinch her tits.

I said, "That was lovely."

After intercourse, I always felt a connection. I loved being with my partner and having them gaze at me in the immediate aftermath, even though it didn't last long. My body confidence peaked at that same moment, which was one of intense joy and pleasure. I always felt really lovely in this moment, even though I knew I was just a looker. And it was the same with this woman who I'd met only a few hours before.

"Did I please you?" I inquired, hoping for confirmation that I had met her expectations.

She played with my hair, grinning.

"More than you can imagine."

"So are girls your thing? Or just an occasional?"

She moved to a more elevated spot on the bed, allowing me to rest my head on her stomach.

She said, "I have a husband."

"He has so many women. He travels and picks them like you and I would pick flowers in the park. I find my own pleasure now."

"Does that bother you?"

I come here sometimes for the females, sometimes for the

lads, because he's dull.

most of the females.

"Well. I'm glad you decided on girls tonight."

I gazed at her legs as I looked down her body. So feminine.

In contrast, I felt like a schoolgirl. And her tidy little bush

was higher up, right in front of my eyes. Shaped and trim,

but also a sign of a grown woman.

"I'm happy too.

There are very few English girls—I can only think of one,

along with the American, of course."

I understood her meaning Hanna right away. And that for

a night, Hanna had once been her purchase. I should have

been jealous, according to conventional wisdom, but

instead it made me feel more connected to them both. I felt weird, like there was no way that we'd both licked this woman's pussy, but it made me feel hotter.

"German girls are more common. But I don't like them much."

I extended my hand and ran my fingers through the scratchy bristles. I had never dated a girl who wasn't smoothed or shaven. It piqued mine.

I questioned, "What's wrong with Germans?"

I turned to face her as she tugged on my collar and said, "Arrogant. They forget they are paid for."

That slightly hurt. A reminder that I was someone's property till the sun rose. She was looking down on me like a slave, telling me to start gratifying her once more.

"Kiss my breasts now.

Give them a mouthful of your lips."

I didn't have any trouble doing that. Huge, solid mounds with such beautiful shapes. I eagerly focused my attention on kissing and caressing them.

I could already feel the urge to cum again.

"Tell me what to do. Tell me how to please you."

I was starting to feel at ease with the notion that all I was was a pleasure object. I desired to be given orders.

When I got out of the club, Hanna was waiting for me outside.

I said, "So, how was he?"

Hannah smiled.

"I'm sore. A fucking machine."

He must have taken something earlier since nobody can pound away for hours on end without cumming.

However, you were a true lady from the start, not just a girlie thing like me."

"First?" I asked, brow furrowing.

"It's paid for first.

additionally older.

Did you enjoy it?

"Well, it was different.

does not imply that I no longer desire you."

I assured her that she had no rivals by leaning in and planting a kiss on her.

"But yeah. It was great. And fucking hell, she paid nearly fifteen hundred for me. Can you believe that?" I said with enthusiasm.

Hanna did not appear surprised, just grinning at my amazement.

"That's Isabella. She's very rich. Everyone around here knows her. Her family owns all the vineyards around the town. There's rumours she bathes in wine."

I saw her lying in the open in a bathtub. White wine cascaded down her tits and covered her entire body.

"Before or after it's bottled?"

"No idea. But imagine that. Drinking wine those massive tits have been washed in."

"I could do that. Those were amazing."

"Not too amazing I hope. I can't compete with those."

"Avoid becoming envious.

For a few hours, they were entertaining to play with, but I want to suck with yours forever."

"Even when they're saggy?"

"Even then."

"Oh look. My two favourite Western girls together."

When we turned back, I don't think any of us expected to see Isabella. And yet there she was, appearing even more foreign against the vivid early-morning light.

Hanna said, unconcerned, "Hi."

"Oh my god."

It stunned me. She was my client, Isabella. Was I using the correct word? I had run out of ideas. I also didn't think I would see her again. Not this soon, for sure.

"It's been a while Hanna."

"It has. But never forgotten."

Her gaze returned to mine.

"And now for your lovely English companion.

So tell me, are the two of you together?

Lovers?

With pride, I said, "Yes."

Hanna, who was standing next to me, accepted my hand and grinned.

"If I'd known, I might have arranged for you to entertain me as a couple."

I said, "Can you do that?"

"Wouldn't you have to bid for the both of us separately?"

Gabriella grinned.

"Anything may be set up at a cost.

Come on over, and I'll buy you some dinner and maybe a

bottle of my delicious wine.

I looked at Hanna, who appeared to be as enthralled with

this rich woman as I was.

"Okay. We'd love to."

She moved to stand between us, and we embraced. so

wasn't actually that much older. As she walked us further

into town, I couldn't help but feel that we were her

daughters, even though she was probably only forty.

We had never eaten at this particular place before. Upon

examining the costs, it was evident why. This was a place

that only wealthy individuals, like Isabella, visited. Most

likely the location where the club bidders congregated prior to their entertainment-filled evening.

As he led us to what he called his nicest table, the waiter recognized her and greeted her by name.

"Please, a bottle of my favorite." she uttered.

"We'll order when my friends have tasted my best juice."

She looked at me, and I smiled as I looked down. As far as I was concerned, only a few hours before, I'd already tasted her greatest juice.

"Perhaps second best."

She had picked her words with more care than I had thought, and my eyes shot up to meet hers.

Next to me, Hanna laughed.

"Don't mind me. I'll make do with the wine."

I turned to face her.

"I don't think it's anything you haven't already

experienced."

My eyes met hers.

"No. No, it's not."

As she turned to face Isabella, I noticed that, amused by our ideas of having licked her pussy, the woman's lips were trying to force a grin.

As the waiter came back, she added, "The wine is all I can offer in public."

"This is a very rare wine."

She carelessly poured the contents of the open bottle among the three glasses, disregarding the occasional spill.

"A unique and challenging vine to grow. Only my vineyard makes the effort here; very few others do anywhere in the world.

I took a sip; I'm not much of a wine expert, and most wines seemed pretty much the same to me, but even I could tell this wasn't anything I'd find in the neighborhood Tesco.

Whoa.

It's that. lovely."

Sipped hers, Hanna.

She exclaimed, "I can taste the grapes."

"This isn't the wine I bathe my massive tits in I should add."

I flushed.

"Have you heard it?"Said Hanna.

"Sorry."

Isabella grinned.

"No big deal. That has been said before. The people in the area often tell stories about me. I believe this to be the contemporary counterpart of the vampire queen wallowing in virgins' blood."

And just to be clear, I don't take a bath in my wine," she

smiled.

She went on, "Or the blood of virgins."

I decided to pick something to eat, so I took up the menu.

Isabella was a lot of fun. extremely clever and loaded with innuendos. There was a deep intelligence and a playful side hiding behind those eyes. I noticed that my liking for her had increased even more than it had when we were sharing a bed.

"As my guests, you must come to the Chateau.

Later on?"

Honestly?

We haven't taken one of the excursions yet, but Hanna mentioned doing one. It would be wonderful if we could come as your guests. Thank you."

I was actually thrilled about the possibility.

"The tour only shows you the vineyards and the presses.

People don't come into the Chateau. That is my private space, and where the real beauty is. Though I am merely a custodian, passing it from one generation to the next. I can't claim credit for its design or even the furniture in it. That appreciation belongs to my ancestors."

The following generation?

Have you got kids?"

She had not struck me as a mother. Maternal, yet not quite a mother. But I guess it was inevitable that she would be. She was old enough, and the rich tend to have a sense of obligation to the past that the common person does not often share. Their estate requires an heir.

"One." she murmured.

Pauline. He is completing his studies in Switzerland. However, he will eventually lead the business procession."

"What about your spouse? Is he not the farm's manager?"

"My side of the family owns it. My spouse works as a

banker. If you want to invest in a solar farm or purchase shares, he is a fantastic choice. However, in regards to wine... He wouldn't be able to tell the difference if I served him a bottle of Vietnamese crap."

During supper, which was a specialty of the area that Isobella suggested, we talked about the history of her farm and how the Germans had used her house during the war.

I felt like I was being evaluated by a queen, but then supper was finished and the bottle was emptied, and Isobella sat back and thought about us.

She stated with a firmness that suggested we couldn't reject, "Tomorrow then."

"Get aboard the bus. On the way, you'll have a fantastic view of the farmland. Midday meals.

We could hang out all day.

And before you drink it, I'll use some wine to wash my tits if you're extremely good."

My mouth dropped open, and I noticed the sly smile that spread across her face as she went for her phone, laughing at me.

Soon after she wrote the text, a flash Mercedes came to pick her up, and I watched her drive away, thinking how lovely it would be to see a little bit of the country, as I had not once left the small town during my original two-week holiday.

"Don't you know she's going to screw us tomorrow?"

I gawked at Hanna.

She asked us to come see her Chateau. And that's it.

Hanna scoffed at my pretend innocence.

"That's not all she wants us to visit."

I knew exactly what Isabella intended, so I wasn't that blind.

Hanna said, tracing a tiny walk over my leg with her

fingers, "She wants a bit of playtime with us together."

I shuddered at the thought.

"Are you comfortable with that?I asked, getting up to go.

"May I ask?"

Hanna compartmentalized sex; for her, this would be compartment number three—fun—but not what we had together. That was separate. I thought about it for a minute before deciding whether or not it was appropriate to answer yes. No.

"Perhaps."

Hanna laughed once more.

"Oh, quit being so sly. Accept it. Sex is incredibly amazing. more so if you just relax and take pleasure in it.

Put your underwear in the drawer. Time will be saved.

Now, I always do. It's what you taught me.

Her fingers darted under my skirt, and I screamed as I

pushed my garments back down and skipped off.

She laughed, "Don't think I haven't noticed."

"Now, how about we go home and get some practice in for tomorrow."

I thought that sounded wonderful.

The bus ride from town was an ancient single-decker that had seen better days before my birth, just like the roads outside town. However, the beauty of the countryside was immediately apparent; Hanna hadn't exaggerated when she'd stated as much when we'd first met.

That took about an hour all the while with Hanna tormenting me; though it was not a very rainy country, the gentle hills were a mass of greenery that stretched to the horizon underneath an almost immaculate blue sky, and off to the right, between the valleys, I saw glimpses of the sea.

She added, "We might do it in the vineyards."

"You can press the grapes with your pussy."

"Shut up."

I took a quick look at the bus. Although it wasn't packed, I didn't want to spend the entire ride writhing on my seat on the verge of an orgasm.

The Chateau was not at all what I had anticipated. brought up with trips to English country houses and pictures of French villas. I had no concept how enormous houses were decorated in different cultures.

It resembled a tiny castle more. Every curve and turret was painted a deep yellow color. The walls were lined with windows with horseshoe arches, and the roofs were made up of domes.

Princess Rapunzel sprang to mind, letting her prince climb up by lowering her incredibly long hair from one of the windows.

"It's beautiful."

I mentioned.

"Like a fairytale."

"Told it was worth a visit. But we get to see inside. The organised trips only visit the vineyards and the pressing rooms. This is as much as you'd see normally."

After getting off the bus, we had a little stroll amid vines that appeared to be loaded with ripening fruits.

"You think these all belong to Isabella?"

"I heard a figure somewhere but can't remember how many acres. But it was a lot. So yeah. I imagine it's everything we can see."

Whoa.

She must be really wealthy."

We were let in by a young maid. Although she didn't seem to speak much English, she recognized us and led the way through the large hallway. There was no ceiling when I looked up. Up to the interior of the dome, it was just endless emptiness. Near the top, where the rooms opened into the space, was a galley.

"I wouldn't want to dust."

Impressive doors with a similar Moorish design led to what I assumed to be the drawing room. Another spacious area that let in plenty of light thanks to tall glass doors on the distant side that were opened to enjoy the wonderful weather in the area.

Isabella looked beautiful. She was reclining on a massive, hefty oak couch. The bench was covered in a rough cream cloth, while the frame and back featured exquisite carvings. The remaining pieces of furniture in the space have a like design.

But Isabella was the one who had my eyes fixed on her. She appeared even more stunning. Elegant and refined in a simple wrap-around skirt and a sash that seemed to teleport her tits into position. Actually, it was tucked tight behind her neck and out of sight beneath lengthy hair.

She stood to greet us and remarked, "Isn't the bus ride a little rickety?"

"I've only seen buses that old in movies." I responded.

Hanna giggled, "You didn't see my school bus."

"That was older than my grandpa."

I asked, "Was it yellow?"

"All school buses are yellow in the States."

Taking our hands, Isabella led the way to a seat.

"You are here. That is what is important. Now come and enjoy a drink."

An additional artistic piece of furniture, generously piled with bottles. Isabella had her spectacles ready to go.

"This wine is blended especially to be refreshing on hot summer days like this."

Hanna remarked, "I love your home."

It was, I believe, the first time I had ever truly witnessed her being overcome by something or someone. Faced with such grandeur, bold, fearless Hanna felt for a minute as small and insignificant as I did.

I inquired, picking up a glass, "Is it just the two of you? You and your husband?"

"Mostly just me. My spouse isn't usually here. Even when he is, he travels and stays in hotels since it's easier for him to entertain his female friends there. I don't mind.

Of course, there are also the servants—a small group of devoted individuals who take care of my home."

"And the vinyards?"

"Local employees. They ride the bus in here every day. I have a group of knowledgeable managers that take care of the vineyard and grape farm for me.

To be honest, I don't know much about the process other

than being able to recognize a good wine. I manage the finances, but other than that, I leave it to them."

"Don't you get lonely on your own?"

"A tiny bit.

That's the reason I bid at the club when I need a little... company.

Don't you think that a straightforward service is so much more honest?

A conversation."

The thought that it had been me providing that simple service less than two days before made me blush.

I muttered, "I suppose so."

She intended to trade money. I got really fixated on something a few weeks back. I can now see what I left behind. Sincerely, she was correct, and it seemed much more equitable. It was truthful.

"And occasionally, I invite special guests to share my home."

I looked at Hanna, who gave me a gentle shove and smiled. Clearly, she saw something in there that I had overlooked.

She showed us around her house with pride. It was an unprecedented level of luxury. And everything with a hint of the bygone era of Spain that still permeated over the border. The town was mostly revivalist. a more contemporary rendition of the building design. This time, it was real.

"This house has been in my family for generations." She stated to us.

"It was built when the vineyards were first planted. And much of the furniture is still from that time."

It just astounded me. A large, vacant house meant for one individual. I noticed a few servants there. They were both young girls in my age range. Isabella sensed the question in my thoughts before I said it.

"I only allow girls in the house. No men. Only my driver is a man and he never comes further than the drive."

"Why?" inquired Hanna.

She probably knew the answer beforehand. All she wanted to do was hear it said.

"Girls are more loyal. They don't tell people what they see."

We arrived at a corridor. It was within the home and had a row of huge doors along one wall, just like the entryway.

They revealed a courtyard beyond. Separated and intimate. Isabella's hand went across my ass and up my back as we made our way through. I merely stared at the view, not reacting. There were wrought iron chairs scattered here and there, and large trees that I didn't recognize provided shelter when the sun was at its highest.

"This is my personal haven; only the house provides

access, so no one may inadvertently stroll in here.

It's very secluded, and I love to sit out here in the afternoon sun."

She demonstrated how much she enjoyed unwinding by spinning and raising her leg while sitting on a bench. Then I noticed her hand bringing her skirt up to her waist. Her bare thighs parted, and the same hand crossed her crotch for a moment.

"No one can see you here, so you can do whatever.

For this reason, I only hire females."

With my mouth hanging open, I wondered whether she would just watch us masturbate. She felt pleasure, closing her eyes and tilting her head back. And I pondered how frequently she did it in the presence of those attendants.

Hanna said in a nearly faint voice, "I'm telling you."

"Before we leave."

I clenched my thighs together, feeling the yearning flow down my legs and into my groin. Hanna seemed excited about it, and I was too, seeing this tiny show.

Isabella simply stopped and got to her feet as like nothing had occurred.

"Let me show you a view out over the land."

After that, she exited through a different door, and we continued around a set of stone stairs. It reminded me like the spire of an old church. There was another spacious, light-filled area at the top. And those arched windows I'd noticed from outside, all around.

"This is a pleasant seating area for early mornings. The bedroom is just over there." She was indicating.

Naturally, it was. When the tour act ended, that was where we were going.

"But here you can see the vines stretching into the distance."

She moved Hanna to the window by placing her hands on her shoulders and then slid down her back to sit on her arse. I watched her take in my friend's aroma with her full breath before turning to smile at me and scrutinizing my face for signs of jealousy. I had none at all. I now understood Hanna's dynamic. She had a liberated soul. but one that I could never forget. I was picking up on being the same quickly.

"Come and see."

We were nearly pressed together in the wide window as she tugged me forward. Beyond, I could see over the hills in even more detail. And the small village was obscured in the distance by a blur of different colors. The water was visible to me too, but the distance and the sun's reflection made it difficult to distinguish where the sea gave way to the sky.

"All this is yours?"

most of what is visible. Sure. We are the nation's biggest farm. Once more, I'm not taking credit. Just now, I serve as the custodian."

Isabella had been scrutinizing our figures while we'd looked at the fields of grapes, but it wasn't until I moved back and saw Hanna still in the window that I understood why she'd kept back. The strong sunshine had made our dresses virtually translucent.

I told her I knew with a cheeky smile and my eyes.

"Perhaps it's time I showed you the bedroom."

I felt a tingle. Hanna was next to me, looking for my hand. She found mine, squeezed it reassuringly, and there was no question left. We were being brought straight into the spider's nest, no disguises at all.

With its bulky wood and elaborately carved headboard that reached up the wall, the bed was the largest I had ever seen, and even in such a large room, it managed to dominate; the layers of luxurious coverings were too many for such a hot country, but here, where the windows looked out onto the shaded side of the house, it was much cooler.

"The early afternoon sun is really intense.

I prefer to come here to unwind and escape the heat."

As I turned, I saw Isabella taking off her garments, starting with the sash and revealing her big bust.

"I like to cool off and have my tension eased away."

The skirt unfolded, her eyes focused on the two of us, and then with a flick, it was gone to one side, leaving me staring at Isabella's nude form for the second time.

She sat on the end of the bed and declared, "I hate clothes."

"I wear them so seldom. However, I felt it would be best if I put something on until you were comfortable."

If she had been nude when we got there, I wondered how I would have responded.

"The two of you look amazing together. Would it be okay if I watched for a little while?"

Hanna took the lead and lifted my dress away while she patted the bed invitingly.

It was exciting and unsettling to have watchful eyes on me as we kissed, but I was also worried because I was displaying nothing to anyone who hadn't seen it before. It was that bizarre blend of feelings and sensations that I should have become used to by now.

I knelt waiting for Hanna to undress and she led me to the bed, passing Isabella who just smiled pleasantly. Those eyes were everywhere, scrutinizing my body, lingering on my pussy.

My knees automatically expanded as fingers reached my pussy. My slit was gripped and pressed, and I felt like I was on fire.

"Uhh."

Her hand grasped my tit, lifting and jiggling it like a stress ball, her fingers staying just free of an aching nipple to agonize me with longing. Then, she started a slow working of my hole while she kissed my neck.

"Mmm."

Isabella drew nearer.

"That is all.

Give your girl what she wants."

I trembled as my moisture turned into a waterfall, drenching Hanna's palm until all motion was stopped.

"So exquisite.

I smell the sex on you. It brings a fresh flavor into the space."

"Uhhh."

I grabbed the bed cover to cover myself as the door opened, staring in dismay at the entrance of a maid who couldn't be any older than Hanna. The maid entered the room with a smile on her face, seemingly unaffected by her employer's nudity or by Hanna lying equally nude on the bed beside me.

The young maid carried the tray in and set it down on the table, and Isabella looked not the least uncomfortable. She thanked the girl and got up to go to the tray, nude and proud, and poured the wine.

I believe that was the moment I realized how similar Isabella and Hanna were to each other: they both accepted their sexuality and didn't feel guilty about it. I decided to let go of my inhibitions and accept sex for what it was. I liked their simple outlook on life and wanted to be just like them. After that, I walked back into the center of the room before the maid closed the door, giving us one last look. I didn't care if she saw me nude or knew what I was going to do; everyone did. There was no reason to hide the truth. Maybe she had even been with Isabella.

Isabella witnessed my epiphany.

Allow yourself to be unbound. My darling little English child, nobody gives a damn.

"Sex should be embraced, not relegated to stuffy Victorian bedrooms."

"I'm learning that."

With a lusty and impatient expression, Hanna sipped her drink and pushed me back toward the bed with my hand.

"Enough speech. You are mine."

I touched her body as I felt myself sliding back, pinching her arse cheeks and forcing them apart for our voyeur to view her crack and the pink tiny hole I'd recently fucked with her dildo. She was at my mouth, kissing and pushing her tongue between my lips with hunger.

After a strong smack that made me startle and caused my flesh to redden, Hanna had me up on all fours with her face at my arse kissing my flesh and riding her tongue along my crack.

"Ooh."

I looked over at Isabella, who had sat down on the side of the room and was staring at us, her knees spread wide, her feet up on the edge of the couch, her fingers running through her bush to gently rub her pussy, droplets of nectar glistening as wet fingers spread it through the coarse hairs.

"Uhh."

My focus returned to Hanna when her finger pierced my ass, making me feel even hotter and determined to make a presentation I could be proud of.

"Tell me why you like fucking Madison."

"Because she has such a tight little butt and a tasty pussy."

Does it become lusciously moist?"

As Hanna licked at my fluids, I trembled from my fingertips to my toes in response.

So damp.

Her cums is like a fountain."

"Uhh."

It was really nice to hear it uttered with such emotion, even if I'm not sure if I was all that horrible.

"And her flavor is so... magnificent. similar to her own soul."

When that finger sank farther into my anus, I twisted my ass against it and saw her tongue licking and sucking my pussy with relish. My eyes rolled to the back of my head.

"Fuck."

"And Madison, how about you?

Does it feel pleasant?"

"Well.

Amazing as hell. The greatest thing ever," I said, my tits jiggling as my voice trembled.

Do you two adore one another?"

We all responded at once.

"Yes."

You two look stunning together. Like two nymphs from heaven."

Isabella decided she had had enough of watching and deliberately approached us, intending to participate in this moment as Hanna had promised she would fuck us.

My head swooned at the gentle fondling, not just the nipples but the entire mound, making me tremble. She knelt in front of me and took my tits in her hands where they hung between my supporting arms. She watched my face as she gently massaged them, squeezing my nipples to leave me weakening.

"Uhh."

"You're sweating."

She kissed my neck, which made me lose even more control over my muscles.

Sweaty girls are my favorite. It facilitates such smooth operation. Very slick."

Hanna threw my pearl into spasms, its tendrils snaking up my spine, making me tremble as we shared a kiss.

"Uhhh."

I lifted my head to look as they grew absorbed in each other right next to where I lay, and then I slipped away as the feelings flowed over me and Hanna switched her focus to Isabella.

Her pink pussy expanded and pressed against Isabella's solid leg, her tits bouncing with every thrust, and Isabella's much larger offerings rolled over her chest. It was fantastic to watch Hanna riding Isabella's thigh like it was a horse.

With Hanna riding her thigh harder, Isabella's pussy was only forward, her own fingers masturbating soft, hot flesh.

For a brief while, I put my fingers to Hanna's pearl, adding fuel to her roaring fire.

"Well. Oh. "Oh."

I moved to sit across Isabella's face, supporting Hanna's neck with my hands as she took ever-deeper gasps, and felt that powerful tongue puncture my hole as our lips touched.

"Uhmm."

My pussy slid across her tongue and my fluids flowed again, soaking her face and greasing it.

Hanna grabbed me firmly with her arms as she had her moment.

"Huh. Fuck it.

I put my lips between Isabella's thighs and ate that hot, excited pussy until she pushed herself away.

"Shit. Sure."

She had been writhing in ecstasy for only a few moments

when her body began to burn from the heat of my mouth and her fingers digging into her flesh.

"Uuuh."

I gave what she said her husband had never done, and she was bucked madly beneath me.

Isabella, and Hanna too, did not give me any break. They turned their attention to me and pushed me onto my back before pulling my ankles.

I wanted nothing more than to offer these two ladies my most intimate, my most sensitive skin, to have them take me to the very peak of my need and push me over the edge so that I sank into the searing inferno of primitive orgasm, while they worked together as I lay with my legs spread wide.

"Oh god."

Two tongues, holding my ankles apart like a chicken's wishbone, each flicking at my pearl.

"Oh my god. Cease."

It was almost intolerable, but the last thing I wanted was for it to end, even though I didn't mean to.

I had no idea how they coordinated so well, but when the two moist muscles met on my pearl again after gliding the length of my slit, I blew up and went completely crazy.

"Fuck."

I gushed, almost to the point of being a squirt, my pussy's juices shooting out into two mouths that were waiting impatiently, like Hanna's fountain.

They kissed me all over, my sperm getting all over their lips.

"Oh fuck."

My eyes darted around the room, seeing nirvana—a luxurious place with exotic furniture and curved walls, a ceiling high above me in the shape of a dome—and never wanting to leave. I wanted that moment of deep satisfaction and release to last an eternity. My head fell back in a daze, unable to comprehend what had just happened to me. My mind was only half functioning.

For a brief minute, all I wanted was to have my hands chained to the large posts while these girls tormented my pussy unceasingly as I noticed the huge headboard above me.

Soon after, the maid returned with more snacks; this time, instead of jumping up or covering myself, I could see that she was well-accustomed to her employer's nudity, as well as that of the other visitors.

She was lighter than most local girls, almost European in look, and I cast a quick check over her sleek shape and expressionless face, wondering if she was serving Isabella more than coffee.

It was almost as if she knew we were done and it became her job to serve us. Three nude ladies, hot and sweaty, covered in cum, and she hardly reacted. This time, she stayed and poured the wine, giving each of us a glass.

I was thrilled that she was seeing me so soon after our intense fucking; I was a hot, sweaty girl with a red face and my hair matted with my partners' sperm. I was proud of my weariness and exhaustion, and I was acutely aware of the mess that only frenzied sex could produce. Suddenly, I liked that someone else could see how satisfying and good the sex had been.

I accepted the offered glass and murmured, "Thank you."

I was still curious about the girl's thoughts as I eyed her tight little ass as she left the room.

"Perhaps I'm missing a new blend."

Isobella brought her glass up and swirled the liquid, catching my attention as I did so.

She tipped the wine onto her tits, still remembering the casual remark about bathing, and let it run into her cleavage, around her nipples, and down to her belly, spreading it with a hand to saturate her flesh until she gleamed with the delicious concoction.

"Not a bath full, but enough to flavour." She said, her mouth hanging out in a smile, as she looked from me to Hanna.

We both moved closer to taste the sweet-tasting fluid from her flesh, deciding we didn't need any more encouragement.

Tell me about the flavor. Do you believe there will be a market for it?"

She filled her body with more wine, tipping it and not caring that it seeped onto the bed covering. My attention was drawn to the part where it collided with her snatch. How it hung in drops and drenched the scratchy hair covering.

I reached down through her bush and slid my tongue

through it.

"Uhh." Isabella gave a gasp.

Hanna came to join me, but she was staring at those tits. I had assumed we were over. Of course not. Once more, I was going to comply with this woman's requests. Her toy was me. Hanna was, too. I also enjoyed it.

By the time I pulled my dress over my head and looked for my shoes, I was completely fatigued.

Isabella remained still. She watched us get dressed while remaining on the bed, content in her nudity.

"Before you leave, I have a suggestion.

Come live with me at the Chateau."

I was shocked to hear that. Hanna seems shocked as well.

"Instead of paying you what you make at the club, I'll give you an allowance. However, the entertainment will be unique. For me.

"What about your husband?"

With a dismissive wave of her hand.

"He is indifferent. He hasn't expressed any desire to touch my body in a very long time. He likes his whores better."

I flushed. To be honest, we were a little more.

"One month." Isabella continued.

A trial run. We can then determine whether this arrangement should be ongoing."

"So we'd be like, more servants?"

I tried not to make it seem obscene or as though I was rejecting the idea as I asked, smiling.

"I guess. but not the same kind. It would be your responsibility to attend to my more private requirements. must make sure that my frustrations aren't taking up my time."

Her meaning was reinforced by the way those fingers

continued to gently caress her pussy.

"You can also spend time alone. On a deeper level, you are lovers. I am aware of that and don't want to ruin what you already have.

Our agreement would be more formal. Like, maybe just at the club, and also with a friend?"

Hanna took my hand in hers.

And that's okay with you? that we would become a pair."

"No."

Hanna confirmed that she still thought we were unique by squeezing my hand. Glancing at me, she searched my face for approval. I gave a quiet nod.

"Okay." Glancing back at Isabella, she said.

"We might let you watch occasionally though."

She was always the one to push the boundaries just a little bit further. I became quite crimson.

"Hanna." I cried out.

I remembered then my little promise to myself to let go of my inhibitions. Recalling that we had started the afternoon with her doing exactly that, I shrugged. observing the two of us.

"All OK. You are welcome to observe."

Gabriella grinned.

"I'd enjoy that." Just on occasion. But you need some alone time. I value that. as long as while we're together, you abuse me.

But you should be aware that I'm a really ravenous woman."

I smiled.

"I don't think that will be a problem."

I had to settle for whoever I could find, whenever I could, back in England. My fingers and a vibrator had been feeding a good desire for the remainder of that period. I've been able to explore my limits and discover that I didn't have any once I met Hanna.

Maybe that's what turned me into an addict, but I had to cum multiple times a day to survive. Really, I could get lost in my want to fuck for the entire day. It was difficult not to want to gaze at Hanna. Isabella would never set a task that I couldn't overcome. Without a question, Hanna was superior to me.

"How do you feel? Hanna queried.

"It's crazy."

It's an absolutely fantastic opportunity. A month. Is that all? For what purpose? doing out our usual tasks."

"And what if we want to stay permanently?"

Would you say that's a poor idea?

Have a look at our future residence. An absolute castle. using attendants.

It will also be a protracted feast."

"Every girl.

Never again a cock." I made a point.

"Anyway, I'm not all that into cock. My preference has always been pussy.

"Okay." I finally expressed what really was thinking.

As the ancient bus rolled closer to us, I gazed out over the rolling hills and valleys. It was really lovely. Very green. And just delightfully toasty.

How much time had passed since I boarded that aircraft at East Midlands airport? Short enough. I was hoping for two weeks in the sun. Maybe a shag with a waiter from the area. I had never envisioned doing the things that I had done. And now, with this wild American girl, I was about to go off on another crazy trip.

"I am content with that. I desire this. as long as we are in unison. like in... in unison."

With a smile, Hanna grasped my hand.

"In any case. We will be in unison. I adore having sex. Anybody. Everywhere. Still, I adore you more. I would never put us in danger."

The bus brakes screeched to a stop, and then there was an audible hiss as the cantilever door clanked open.

"Then it's a yes." I verified.

"Let's do it."

We can verify it later by giving Isabella a call. I ascended the staircase and found a seat on the bus.

That's it, then. That's how I went from being a typical office lady in gloomy England, fucking two gorgeous women multiple times a day, to living in a castle in paradise.

Isabella was a queen of exoticism. Very beautiful indeed. She made us serve her. Neither did we clean or cook. That was why she had servants. We used to work in the bedroom for our employer. or somewhere else she felt drawn to. It wasn't difficult to fuck her; she paid us to do it. Under different circumstances, we would have cheerfully done it for free, but we also had our futures in mind. Even in nirvana, money was a reality from which one could never truly escape.

We would have nothing save the savings we had up until we were too elderly to continue on. We would eventually need to rely on that to sustain ourselves as we aged together in this paradise. And as much as I cherished holding Isabella's body in my arms and feeling her tits between my fingers, I knew that I would always be with Hanna. However, old age wouldn't come about for a while.

We were Isabella's harem for the time being. Her willing, private playthings. Our lifestyle was one of extravagance and revelry. I was having a great time the entire time.

Nothing is more joyful than when you finally get together.

And I couldn't express how grateful I was for my good

fortune that I could enjoy it multiple times a day, every day,

without feeling anxious or stressed.

Acknowledgments

The Glory of this book's success goes to God Almighty and my beautiful Family, Fans, Readers & well-wishers, Customers, and Friends for their endless support and encouragement.

About The Author

I've spent nearly a decade penning romantic novels. As a passionate writer of erotica, I craft dark, romantic erotica. Anime Naked Truth Se of Sacred Sexuality: Forbidden Seducing Short Stories of an Erotica Nude Sexy Girl Poster. Alongside Erotic Mystery Fiction, Victorian Erotica Sex, Black & African American Erotica, Euthanasia, Daddy Teaching, Forced Domination, Alpha Monster Cuckold, and BDSM for Adults, there's an Erotic Fiction in Kinky Family. I write dark, sensual romance because I adore the power of darkness and everything that it entails. Romance novels have always been my favorite kind of books, and now I'm writing them. The idea that you will like reading and enjoying my fiction as much as I enjoy pushing the frontiers of sexual pleasure in my writing thrills me more than anything else.